SHADOW OF THE LEOPARD

SHADOW OF THE LEOPARD

HENNING MANKELL

annick press
toronto + new york + vancouver

PUBLISHED IN THE U.S.A. BY
Annick Press (U.S.) Ltd.

DISTRIBUTED IN CANADA BY
Firefly Books Ltd.
66 Leek Crescent
Richmond Hill, ON
L4B 1H1

DISTRIBUTED IN THE U.S.A. BY
Firefly Books (U.S.) Inc.
P.O. Box 1338
Ellicott Station
Buffalo, NY 14205

Annick Press Ltd.
First published by Rabén & Sjögren, Bokförlag, Sweden, 2007,
as *Eldens Vrede*
First English edition published by Allen & Unwin, Australia,
2009, as *The Fury in the Fire*

Copyedited by Geri Rowlatt
Proofread by Paula Ayer
Cover and interior design by Irvin Cheung/iCheung Design, inc.
Cover illustration by Shelagh Armstrong

Cataloging in Publication
Mankell, Henning, 1948–
    Shadow of the leopard / Henning Mankell ; translated by
Anna Paterson.

Translation of: Eldens vrede.
ISBN 978-1-55451-200-3 (bound).—ISBN 978-1-55451-199-0
(pbk.)

    I. Paterson, Anna II. Title.

PZ7.M334Sh 2009   j839.73'74   C2009-902543-4

Printed and bound in Canada

Visit our website at **www.annickpress.com**

BEFORE THIS STORY BEGINS

TEN YEARS HAVE PASSED SINCE I first started to tell the story of Sofia, a girl from Mozambique, in a book called *Secrets in the Fire.* When Sofia was nine years old, she lost both her legs in a terrible landmine explosion that killed her ten-year-old sister Maria.

A few years later I wrote another book about Sofia and her family. It was called *Playing with Fire* and was mostly about Sofia falling in love for the first time in her life. But it was also about the despair she felt when her older sister Rosa fell ill with AIDS and died.

Then, five years ago, I promised to write one more story about Sofia. Much has happened in my life and in Sofia's, too. Now I feel the time has come for another book about her.

In the books about Sofia I mix truth and invention. What I describe has happened in reality, but not exactly in that way. Very often stories grow out of combinations of reality with dreams, or imagined events. Sofia's life merges with the lives of other people, as I borrow from their fates.

I have read this story aloud to Sofia. We spent a few warm African evenings together, talking by a camp fire. She listened to my story and now I'll tell it to you, who hold this book in your hand...

Henning Mankell

Sofia is running. It is dark. She must hurry and she's very frightened. She doesn't know why she runs, or to where, or why she's afraid. Something terrifying is after her, something dangerous and evil. It is catching up to her.

Sofia runs on through the night, alone and very scared...

SOFIA KEPT HER EYES CLOSED as she remembered. This nightmare had haunted her for ten years, ever since a terrible landmine explosion had killed her sister Maria and injured Sofia. Sofia's legs had been torn off and her body had been badly burned.

Then Sofia shook herself and opened her eyes. She threw a few more branches on the fire. All that had happened ten years ago. She was almost twenty now.

It was late, but she was still outside, sitting on a straw mat by the fire. Most evenings she would have been asleep already. Tonight she couldn't sleep. Behind her, inside the small mud-brick house, the rest of her family slept.

She could hear Mama Lydia's heavy snoring. Now and then one of the sleeping children whimpered.

Sofia's dog, Lokko, was lying opposite her, on the other side of the fire. His head was resting on his paws, but whenever Sofia moved, or an insect fluttered too close to his nose, Lokko looked up and caught her eye.

Sofia sometimes felt that meeting the dog's gaze was as strange as staring straight into the fire, where the flames danced and the burning wood crackled, throwing sparks into the night air. Lokko's eyes were like mouths of caves where unknown things were hiding in the shadows.

Images danced in the flames…

All around her the village slept. She heard a child cry in the dark distance. She listened. The child sounded sick, feverish.

The sound hurt her deeply. She had two small children of her own and feared the crying that might be a warning of illness to come. You could never know. She had seen too many children die of fever, or diarrhea, or malaria. Because everyone in her village was poor, nobody was sure that there would be a doctor to help them, or enough money to pay for medicines.

The sad child was silent now. Using one of her crutches, Sofia moved a few logs into the fire. Lokko watched her.

"Isn't it pretty?" she whispered. "Look, the flames

are jumping and dancing. I was just the same once…I could dance, too."

Lokko's large eyes were fixed on her.

"I wonder what you're thinking," Sofia said. "If only you could talk to me and tell me what goes on inside your head."

Sofia put the crutch down, leaned back against the wooden stool she used as a backrest, and listened to the silence, wondering what it might mean not to be a child any longer. I'm a grown-up now, all of a sudden.

Then she let her thoughts wander back in time, along a well-traveled path in her mind, which grew longer for every day she lived. Perhaps one day it would be too long, and she too old and too tired to follow it to the end.

It took her, as always, to Maria and Rosa, her two dead sisters who were waiting for her at different places along the path. She'd met her father, Hapakatanda, as well. He had died when she was too young to remember much of him.

Suddenly, it seemed as if she were no longer alone. Others were sitting by the fire, shadowy figures who had gathered near her. All were children, all girls, but of different ages. And all were Sofia's younger selves! She could reach out her hand and say hello to herself as a half-grown girl or a toddler, almost too little to walk on her own.

What was her very first true memory? Probably the

time when her Mama had brought her along to the river. Sofia had been playing on the bank while Ma Lydia and the other women were doing the laundry. They were up to their knees in the water, bending over to scrub the clothes. Sofia knew that there were dangerous animals in the river. Crocodiles might come sneaking along, with only their eyes showing above the surface, and strike in an instant. Their huge jaws could grab people and drag them under. Lydia and the other women were always on the alert. The crocodiles were cunning and you never knew when they were around.

Suddenly a croc had broken cover, its sharp teeth glittering in its enormous, wide-open mouth. Its jaws snapped shut around the arm of one of the women. Before anyone could react, she was pulled underwater. She had come back up just once. Sofia could still remember the sound of her scream. Then she vanished. No one ever found any trace of her.

My life's first memory, Sofia thought. Seeing someone get attacked by a wild animal and die. It frightened her.

A mosquito landed on her arm and Sofia slapped it before it had time to start sucking her blood.

OTHER REMEMBERED IMAGES CAME TO MIND and faded again. Maria was part of almost every one of them. Even though they were poor, and Ma Lydia sometimes wept because she couldn't feed her children, Sofia felt

———

that a special light shone over her childhood.

Until that awful morning that changed her entire life.

Sofia truly didn't want to think about what had happened, but couldn't stop herself.

It was early in the morning and the sun had just risen above the horizon. They were running along the path. Every morning, Ma Lydia would warn them to stick to the paths and never step onto land where no one walked. Bad things lurked there, small earth-crocodiles that could open their jaws and tear arms and legs off little children.

At first, both girls were running, but then Sofia started jumping on one leg. Maria stopped. Sofia jumped on her left foot and had to put her right foot down to get back on the path.

She remembered nothing else, only a searing pain and a vast, black silence.

In the hospital, their beds had been placed side by side. Both of them had been very badly hurt. One night, Maria reached for Sofia's hand, held it, and said, "I'll go home now." Her eyes closed. In that moment, Sofia knew that Maria had died.

Sofia's eyes filled with tears. She could see Maria standing on the path, Maria in her white dress, laughing. The huge difference between life and death could sometimes seem so small.

She wiped the tears from her eyes. If Maria had lived, she would have been almost twenty-one and perhaps a mother, too. Sofia tried to visualize her sister as a grown-up, but it was impossible. She could imagine Maria with the round hips and breasts of a woman, but her face was that of a laughing child. However many years passed, Maria would always stay a child.

Sofia shaded her eyes from the dazzling firelight to look at the starry night sky. Her father had told them that people who died turned into stars. She thought it hard to believe, though the idea that Maria was glittering up there was beautiful.

Lokko got up, scratched himself, and disappeared into the darkness. Sofia sipped cold tea from a plastic mug and listened for sounds from the house. Ma Lydia sometimes snored so loudly you could hear her through the walls, but not just now. Lydia slept on a straw mat on the floor with one thin, small pillow under her head. Sofia kept asking her if they should buy her a bed, but Lydia said no every time. She had always slept on the floor.

Was Lydia getting old? Lydia herself didn't know how old she was. There was no record. Lydia's mother, who had given birth eleven times, couldn't remember. Her father thought her birthday was in the autumn, one year when the rains had been very heavy. Sofia guessed that her Ma was about forty-five years old, though so tired and worn she looked older.

———

Had the deaths aged her? Lydia had lost four of her seven children: Maria, her older daughter Rosa, and two little sons, one from malaria and another from a stomach illness.

Lydia had wept despairingly over her children and the tears had worn deep furrows in her face. Grief had entered her body and turned into pain in her joints, in her arms and legs. No wonder her face and body had aged.

Lokko emerged out of the dark and lay down by the fire again. Sofia kept wondering about the past. Why was it the way it was? Why had Maria died and not Sofia? Why not the other way around? Was this what being adult meant? Realizing that there were no answers and that you had to put up with things as they happened?

Like the year when Rosa had been ill and died, late one night. Her family had been sitting around her, holding onto her tight to stop her from leaving them. She died all the same.

Sofia and Lydia usually walked to the graves once a week. The village burial ground was on a slope above a small stream. Every time, more holes would have been dug and more dead bodies lowered into them. And almost every time, Lydia crouched down and wept, as if her children had died just recently. They were always present in her mind.

Sofia felt sure that the living could talk with the dead. Sometimes she sensed that Maria and Rosa and her little dead brothers, too, were close by and that they were whispering to each other. You whispered with the dead. Sofia couldn't quite tell why that should be.

Did the dead talk with each other? Did Rosa and Maria whisper together, or was it silent down there, under the ground?

Sofia looked up at the stars and, once again, thought that being an adult meant being at a loss for so many answers.

SHE NEEDED TO GO TO THE TOILET and hauled herself upright with her crutches. If she sat on the ground for too long, her hips started aching. Lokko followed her. He never left her alone and kept an eye on everyone in the family, especially Sofia's two little ones.

She crouched down to pee. Afterward, as she straightened up, her hips hurt again. Once she had settled by the fire, she stoked it and watched the flames flare up. The burning wood smelled a little like the perfume Rosa sometimes used.

Now, the glowing embers seemed to form into her dead sister's face. Rosa had been one of the loveliest girls Sofia had ever seen. There had been times when she felt envious of her big sister, who was so beautiful that all the boys hung around her. But when she was dying, she had become too thin to stand by herself and her skin was stretched tightly over her bones.

Everyone dreaded AIDS too much to want to talk about it. It made you very thin and ill, and then you died. Everyone, except possibly the very old, could catch it and no one had a cure, not even the city hospital doctors.

Sofia's thoughts were interrupted by the sound of someone walking along the road. Actually, Lokko had heard the steps first. His ears pricked up and he was suddenly alert. Who could it be, this late at night?

Then Sofia saw it was old Augustino on one of his walks. He was one of the oldest people in the village, an outsider who lived alone in a half-ruined hut. He dressed oddly and kept muttering incomprehensibly all the time. When he couldn't sleep, he would walk around in the village instead. He was a kindly soul and no one was scared of him.

Sofia had spoken to Augustino once when she too had been sleepless. As she half listened to him rambling on, she had suddenly grasped that he was trying to explain to her why he walked at night. It was to look for fallen stars. If you had the right kind of eyes, he said, you could spot them glowing faintly on the ground.

Augustino stopped to look up at the sky. Then he spotted Sofia by the fire and waved to her. She waved back, hoping that he wouldn't come closer and start talking. She wanted to be alone with her thoughts. He must have understood, because he kept on walking and was soon swallowed up by the darkness. Lokko settled down again, with his head resting on one of his paws.

Sofia yawned. She was tired, but wanted to stay by the fire for a little longer.

Their house had two small rooms. They cooked over a fire in a fireplace in a separate shed. The toilet and the place where you washed were outside the house, too, hidden behind straw mats hanging from poles. Lydia and Sofia's two brothers slept in one room, and Sofia and her two children in the other. In that room, Sofia also kept her sewing machine: her pride and joy. During all the bad years, it had given her a way to earn a little money to help feed and clothe the family.

Sofia felt warm inside at the thought of her sleeping family. I have a mother and I have brothers. And my two children are both healthy and have eaten before bedtime, she said to herself. Every day, when I know they're sleeping and not hungry, I feel life is worth living. If I had died, my children would not have existed.

Sometimes, she thought that her children were her sisters' children, too, that in a way they had three mothers.

She smiled, yawned again, and felt another pain in her stomach. Maybe she really was pregnant again. Tomorrow she'd walk to the health center to find out. She put her hand on her belly, closed her eyes, and tried to sense if she was or wasn't. The two earlier times, she had felt sure that the baby was there before it had been confirmed, but not now.

———

She leaned back against the stool and hummed a tune, a song for children, which she and Maria used to sing together. Her mood was a strange mixture of sadness and happiness. Maybe feeling both at the same time might be another sign of having grown up.

There were some of her diaries, notebooks with red covers, lying next to her on the mat. She had woken up one morning knowing that this writing was what she had to do, and set out to travel all the way to the city to find the right shop. Ever since Rosa died, she had filled page after page. Now she opened one of the books at random and leaned closer to the fire to read.

"Moon Boy." Sofia smiled. Once, it had been her name for Armando, who would become the father of her children.

"Moon Boy." She looked through the book, stopping now and then to read in the fading light. Imagine, she had called him "Cinnamon Boy," too. She remembered the night when he had come to the house. He wanted to see her, he said, just to say, "Thank you for mending my pants."

She closed the diary. It seemed so long ago. At the time, Rosa was severely ill and close to death. Sofia had been almost paralyzed with grief, but she had started to fall in love with Armando.

Now they had two children together and a third might be on the way. The fire had died down. She could hardly make out the shape of Lokko where he was lying on the other side of the cooling ashes. She closed her eyes and yawned again. Time for bed.

As usual, Lydia was the first to wake. When she stepped outside in the early dawn, stretching her sore joints, she discovered Sofia asleep on the straw mat by the cold fire. Some of her diaries lay beside her. Lydia looked lovingly at her sleeping daughter, at her artificial legs and the crutches. Then she woke Sofia, shaking her gently until her eyes opened.

"Where am I?" Sofia asked.

Lydia smiled.

"You've been sleeping outside, by the fire."

Sofia sat up. In the distance, Mrs. Mukulela's bad-tempered rooster had started crowing. A new day had begun.

2

SOFIA WAS THE ONLY ONE in the family who wore a small watch strapped to her wrist. She had sewn a skirt for one of Armando's sisters, who worked in a city café and earned good money. When she had come to get her new skirt, she noticed Sofia eyeing her watch. The clock face was black, with yellow hands, and it had a red plastic strap.

"If you like, you can have the watch instead of money," she said.

Sofia's face went hot and she felt bad about that. Blushing was something children did. She was behaving like a little girl who couldn't handle anything unusual. But Armando's sister noticed her embarrassment and just laughed nicely. Sofia calmed down.

"I'd like the watch, please."

"Do you know how to tell the time?"

This made Sofia angry. Of course she knew how to tell the time. One of the nurses in the hospital had taught her.

"The skirt is lovely. Here, you have my watch. The battery is tiny, but lasts for a whole year."

From then on, Sofia wore it every day. She amused herself by trying to guess the right time before she'd allow herself to check the watch. After a while she nearly always got it about right, even at night.

Now it was ten past seven. Everyone in the village would have woken up, but Mrs. Mukulela's rooster kept crowing all the same. Ma Lydia heated what was left of the soup from yesterday's supper and served it up for the children, both her own and Sofia's.

Sofia took the chance to leave while they were all busy eating. If the children spotted her walking down the main road through the village, they'd start to cry, wanting her to be there for them. Sofia had once asked if she too had made a fuss when Ma Lydia went away. Had she howled like that?

"Every time," Ma Lydia replied. "You used to make a bigger noise than any of your brothers and sisters."

Although it was early morning, the sun was already high in the sky. Soon Sofia was sweating. As always, it started on her forehead, just below the hairline, and on the skin between her breasts, and then her back grew damp, too. She walked on. There is nothing you can do about the sun.

She needed both crutches this time. If the walk was short, she could manage with one, but the health center was six kilometers, almost four miles, away. Thinking about something special helped to make the time pass and today it would be Armando, the first and only love of her life. One night, seven years ago, he had stood in the road, the moon bathing him in blue light.

Off and on, he would come along and ask to see her. They would sit together in the shade behind the house. But she kept their talks short, terrified that he might become bored with her and think that she cared more for her two dead sisters than for him. She seemed to have little space left for happiness and couldn't be any different. Being in love had to wait.

Six months passed before the joy of seeing Armando come walking along the road began to occupy her thoughts more than anything else.

A year later, he moved in with them. Armando and Sofia slept in the inner room, Lydia and the two boys in the other one. Lydia liked Armando, though she had been doubtful at first. But he worked and didn't drink too much beer, so she decided that Sofia had found a good man.

That he had a job was of course very, very important. Armando worked as a car mechanic in the small repair shop at the edge of the village. The mechanics spent most of their days keeping two old tractors going. After a year or so, Armando came home one day and told them that the repair shop was about to close. He would have to travel to the city and look for work. Sofia was pregnant with their first child, and she felt frightened. What if Armando remained unemployed, or even disappeared in the city? But after a few weeks, he landed a job. He came home every weekend, only going back to the city late on Sunday nights.

Once, Sofia had traveled to the city to see him. His job was in a small engineering workshop that overflowed into the street. The owner was an elderly man called Samuel, whose almost toothless mouth often widened in a broad smile. Samuel couldn't afford to pay good wages, but Armando liked him all the same. He knew he was lucky to find any kind of job and wouldn't dare to leave without first having found one with better pay.

Sofia recalled the birth of her baby, Leonardo. She had woken early one morning because her waters had broken. They knew that her time would soon come and had arranged that Mrs. Mukulela's nephew would drive Sofia to the health center in his old truck. Lydia sent one of the boys, who ran along the road as fast as his legs could carry him through the dust. Sofia's belly was heaving and pulsating. Despite her many pregnancies, Ma Lydia seemed more anxious than if she herself had been about to give birth again. When the man with the truck arrived, she shouted at him and bossed him about. They lifted Sofia into the passenger seat and Lydia climbed up on the back, where a couple of goats had been tethered.

———

They made it to the health center in time. Doctor Nkeka was ready and waiting. He was the doctor who had told Rosa that she had caught a deadly disease. He smiled when he saw Sofia. He had examined her twice during her pregnancy and told her that she was in good shape.

"That's my girl!" he said, when he came to meet her. "You're neither too early nor too late."

BABY LEONARDO WAS BORN two hours later. Ma Lydia was with Sofia all the time and held her hand when the labor pains grew more intense. Sofia didn't want to cry out, not even at the worst pains. She felt she had done enough screaming when she was in the hospital after the landmine accident. Then, the pain had been so bad she had sometimes fainted in the middle of a scream. Giving birth to her baby had to be different.

Lydia was the first to see that the newborn was a boy. Tears began streaming down her cheeks.

"Sofia, you have a son," she said.

Sofia took her baby from Doctor Nkeka and thought he looked just as ugly and wrinkled as other newborns she had seen. But he was the most wonderful creature she could ever have imagined.

"Maria," she whispered. "Maria, Rosa! Look at him!"

"He is beautiful," Doctor Nkeka said. "And the birth was perfectly normal. All is well. What will you call your little boy?"

Lydia was sitting on a stool by the bed, rocking from side to side from sheer happiness. Sofia kept looking at her while she tried to think of a reply. She realized that she hadn't given a thought to the child's name. Armando hadn't mentioned anything either.

"I don't know," Sofia said.

"A fine boy should have a fine name," Doctor Nkeka told her.

THE FOLLOWING DAY, Armando turned up and found Sofia and her new baby already back home. Doctor Nkeka, who lived in the city, had stopped by the repair shop with the news of the birth and Samuel had given Armando a day off. When he bent over his son, Sofia saw him as Moon Boy once again.

"Hold him," Sofia said.

Armando shook his head. "I don't dare."

"He's your son!"

"I'm scared I might drop him."

Ma Lydia was standing outside the house and heard them through the open window. She came in at once and looked sternly at Armando.

"Of course you must hold your son," she said. "You won't drop him."

While Sofia watched Lydia put the baby in Armando's arms, she thought of Maria and Rosa again. Could they see her now, although she couldn't see them? Naming a baby girl would have been so easy. She would have been called Maria. And the next girl would have been Rosa.

But what to call this baby boy?

"He must have a name," Sofia said. "What do you think we should call him?"

"Rogerio, like my father," Armando said.

"It's a good name. But he's no Rogerio, somehow. He's another person."

Sofia noticed that Armando was a little disappointed, but he didn't protest. What mattered most to her was his awkward happiness at seeing their baby.

She felt shy and awkward herself. How could she be responsible for this child? Until now, she too had been a child. And she was still disabled.

In the evening, when Armando had left to go back to the city, Sofia lay awake for a long time after the baby had fallen asleep. She never tired of watching the face of this new person, who by then had been part of her world for two days and, soon, two nights.

With a sudden sadness, she realized that the baby might one day be ashamed of his mother, who took off her artificial legs and put them next to her bed every evening. She chased the anxious thought away. The boy would, after all, have a normal, healthy father.

Lydia came into the room to look at the sleeping baby. The house had no electricity, but a burning candle stood on a stool next to Sofia's bed.

"Are you happy?" Lydia asked.

"I'm very happy," Sofia said. "But frightened. I'm afraid that he'll die."

"He won't die," Lydia told her. "He looks strong. And if he gets sick, we'll take him to see Doctor Nkeka right away."

When Lydia had left, Sofia blew out the candle and tucked in the mosquito net. There were mosquitoes in the room. She wasn't going to risk them stinging her baby and perhaps infecting him with malaria.

She dozed in the dark room. Then, suddenly, one of Doctor Raul's stories came back to her and she opened her eyes. Doctor Raul had cared for her after her accident. He usually turned up late at night before going home from the hospital. Sometimes, when he was very tired, he'd just sit down on the edge of her bed and ask her how she was. He wouldn't say anything more, only listen to her reply. But on other evenings, when he was less exhausted, he told her stories about people and what went on the world.

Once, he had described a strange man who, many hundred years ago, had invented a machine that could fly. What was the man's name? Sofia had thought his name was beautiful and now she wanted to remember. Irritably, she racked her brain to make it recall what that extraordinary man had been called.

It was hopeless. She cautiously turned to lie on her

———

side, pulled the baby close to her breast, and had almost fallen asleep when the name flew toward her out of the darkness.

Leonardo!

That was it. She lit the candle again to look at her baby.

"Leonardo," she whispered. "That's your name. And when you're an adult, everyone will know why Leonardo was the only right name for you."

SOFIA STOPPED WALKING ALONG THE ROAD and wiped the sweat off her brow. The memory of how "Leonardo" had come to her still made her feel happy. When she had told Armando, he too had liked the name.

Sofia stopped where the road swung past her old school. It was a low, brown building without doors or windows. She watched the children playing outside. How quickly time had passed! It didn't seem long since she had played there, too. Strange, she thought. You never know what's waiting for you along the road.

She started walking again. Her thoughts wandered back to the birth of her second child. Maria was born two years after Leonardo.

Sofia had suggested her name one evening when they were sitting by the fire. At the time, Sofia's belly was so big she could hardly move.

"Lydia. It begins with an *L*," Armando said. "And

Leonardo, too. What if we have another boy? Or if it's a girl?"

They spent the evening playing with names.

"Laurinda," Armando went on. "Or Lucas."

"Maria," Sofia had said. "If it's a girl."

It was a girl. And they called her Maria because there could be no other name for her. So Sofia, not yet twenty, had two children, one toddler and a newborn girl. Armando was still working for Samuel, Mrs. Mukulela's rooster kept crowing in the mornings, and Sofia often thought that, though they were poor, she wouldn't ever wish to change the way she lived.

When Armando came home on a Saturday, she rested calmly at night, close to him in the narrow bed. Armando was always very tired when he came back from the city, but despite that they talked a lot about their future together. Their most precious dream was that the children would go to school. In his short time at school, Armando had scarcely done more than learn to read and write. Sofia had stayed on for longer. She had held onto a dream of learning more and, in some wonderful, unfathomable future, studying to become a doctor. As time passed, she grew doubtful. If she were to study at the university she'd have to move to the city. How would she find the courage? And the money? What about her legs? Maybe she should aim at becoming a teacher instead.

———

Besides, she was responsible for Lydia and her younger brothers. Lydia had changed a great deal after Rosa's death. When Rosa was alive, Lydia laughed easily and seemed able to keep working forever. Something tore inside her when her eldest daughter died. She didn't like talking about her feelings and Sofia never asked any direct questions, but kept a watchful eye. It would be wrong to leave her before the boys had grown up. And who would look after Lydia when she was too old to walk to the fields every morning and hoe the long rows under the burning-hot sun until darkness fell?

SOFIA FINALLY ARRIVED AT THE HEALTH CENTER and stopped in the shade of a tree to wipe the sweat from her face and chest. When she leaned forward to reach under her blouse, she thought her breasts were surely big enough to make plenty of milk for a new baby.

If the baby was to be a girl, her name would be Rosa. If not, Armando could decide.

Sofia crossed the sandy entranceway, where people sat with cloths over their heads to protect themselves from the merciless sun. Many were moaning. Sofia hurried past them on her crutches. Just now, she couldn't cope with other people's misery.

The waiting room was crowded. The air was stale and heavy, despite the two open windows. Sofia leaned against the wall and shifted her weight to the crutches.

A young man, who looked feverish, rose on trembling legs to make room for her on the wooden seat. She shook her head. Standing was all right.

Her gaze wandered over the sick people in the room. Everyone is afflicted by something, she thought. No one escapes either illness or grief.

It took almost an hour before Sofia could see Doctor Nkeka. She noticed at once that he was tired. Too many patients today.

He observed Sofia while cleaning his glasses.

"Sofia," he said. "How are you?"

"I'm fine, thank you."

"And your children?"

"Fine."

"Your mother, how's she? Remind me of her name."

"It's Lydia. She's well, too."

Doctor Nkeka put the glasses back on his nose and nodded thoughtfully.

"It's a rare thing to hear that so many people are well. Especially where I'm sitting. All day long I listen to sad people telling me about their hurt and pain and their fears. But you're just fine. So, why are you here?"

"I think I might be pregnant," Sofia mumbled.

Doctor Nkeka leaned toward her.

"Pregnant? Well, well. We'll soon know for sure."

He banged with a stick on a door and a nurse opened it immediately.

——

"Sofia here wants to find out if she's pregnant," he said. "Let's see if we can help her."

Sofia knew the routine: she had to pee into a small bowl and the nurse would test the urine. She felt tense and it took quite a while before she could squeeze out a few drops. Then she left the cubicle and handed over the bowl.

"Do you want to have a baby?" the nurse asked her.

"Yes," Sofia answered. "I really do."

"Would it be your first child?"

"No. I've got two already."

"Do you earn enough money? Can you afford to feed them all?"

"Yes, I can."

The nurse nodded, put a test paper into the sample, and soon took it out again.

Sofia looked at its color. She *was* pregnant! A great joy flowed over her, like a warm shower. Lydia would be so happy, and Armando, too. Armando!

The nurse opened the door to Doctor Nkeka's room.

"Sure enough, Sofia is pregnant!" she sang out cheerfully.

"Come back for a checkup a few months from now," Doctor Nkeka called to her. "Just to make sure you're all right. And after the baby is born I don't want you back in my clinic because it has malaria."

"I've got a mosquito net," Sofia called back to him.

Sofia walked home. The sun baked the top of her head, but life seemed so easy now. She didn't even feel any pain in her hips, despite the long walk.

Something great had touched her. It wasn't simply that she was going to have another baby. She felt invulnerable.

Nothing could hurt her now.

She was in a hurry. There was much to talk about. First of all, she wanted to tell Lydia. The next day, Armando would come home.

Then he'd learn the big news.

———

3

LATER, SOFIA WOULD ALWAYS THINK of the months that followed as "the good time." As she remembered it, she was often happy and the only thing that troubled her was her sore back. Now and then it ached so badly she could hardly move and she could be irritable then, with the boys and sometimes with Ma Lydia. It could also happen that she took her bad temper out on her own children and even Armando.

"Why get mad at us?" he'd ask.

"I can't stand on the side of the road and give whoever comes by first a hard time, can I?"

He didn't always see it her way, and they wouldn't be on speaking terms when they crawled into their narrow bed. Then they'd forget about it, until the next time Sofia lost her temper.

SOFIA GAVE BIRTH TO HER BABY eight months after Doctor Nkeka had confirmed that she was pregnant. The births of Leonardo and Maria had been painful, and the doctor had thought it might have something to do with her injuries. This time it was much easier, though.

It was a baby girl. When Sofia saw her for the first time, she thought the little wrinkled bundle even looked like Rosa. It was as if her sister had returned.

Lydia had hurried along to Sofia's bedside. When she came back from the city, where she had been selling vegetables at the market, the boys had been very excited and told her that Sofia had gone to the health center.

Lydia was quite breathless and her face was covered in sweat.

"Ma, it's a girl."

"Is she all right?"

Sofia showed off her baby.

"Look, ten fingers and ten toes. And she has two eyes, two ears, a mouth, and a nose. And hair all over her head and the usual things between her legs."

"Thank goodness," Lydia said and sat down on the edge of the bed.

"Her name will be Rosa," Sofia told her mother.

Lydia's eyes grew moist, but she said nothing.

TWO DAYS LATER, it was Saturday and Armando came home. Lydia and the boys went off to meet him. The children talked at the same time in their eagerness to tell him what the new baby looked like. Armando nearly ran the rest of the way, shouting to everyone he met that he had a new daughter. Some people weren't all that impressed.

"Shame it wasn't a boy."

"Nothing wrong with daughters," Armando shouted back.

Sofia was waiting for him, sitting on the steps. She had taken care to dress nicely and was cradling the baby in her arms. Armando wasn't only meant to look at his new daughter, but also to notice Sofia and see what an attractive mother she was, despite her artificial legs and her plump body.

Armando stopped in front of her, a little shy.

"Is everything all right?" he asked.

"Everything was fine. And quick. It didn't even hurt all that much."

"Did you bleed a lot?"

Now it was Sofia's turn to feel a little uncomfortable. It was rare for her and Armando to talk about these things.

"Not much," she mumbled.

Then Sofia folded back the shawls that hid the baby's face and held her up for Armando to see. He leaned forward cautiously. The boys wanted to see, too, and were making a fuss, but Lydia kept them away.

"She's just as wrinkly as the others," Armando said.

"New babies look like that," Sofia replied crisply.

"But she's a very pretty baby!"

"I want her name to be Rosa."

"That's fine with me. Does she cry much?"

"Only when she's hungry. Do you want to hold her?"

Armando wiped his hands on his pant legs and picked up the baby carefully, as if she were made of glass.

"Look, her funny little face," he said. "But you can see already she'll be lovely when she grows up."

"Like Rosa. You wouldn't really know. Rosa was so ill when you saw her."

THAT EVENING, SOFIA AND LYDIA sat talking by the fire. Armando slept, tired out after his tough week struggling to fix wrecked cars. Mrs. Mukulela was walking past, but stopped and sat down to talk. She smelled of beer and laughed loudly at everything anyone said.

After a while, she wandered off down the road and disappeared into the darkness.

"She drinks far too much," Lydia said grimly. "And I don't know where she picks up the men she drags home with her."

"Oh, leave her alone," Sofia replied. "She's laughing, so her life can't be that bad, surely?"

Lydia stirred the fire with a stick. Sparks flew up into the night air.

"I hope you have another son," she said. "Then I can die in peace."

Surprised, Sofia looked at her.

———

"Why do you say that?"

"Because no one ever knows how long life will last. And I think you'd need one more son to support you when you grow old."

"Ma, are you sick?"

"Nothing worse than usual."

"I don't want you to die. Our family has seen enough deaths. The rest of us had better stay alive. Besides, there are the children to care for."

"I'm not planning to die. I can cope with a few more years. But you must realize that I'm growing old."

"You're only forty-three," Sofia said. "Or maybe forty-four or forty-two. Perhaps forty-five."

"I feel old. My arms and legs ache. I can't work as hard as I used to."

"You could live to twice your age. I want you to grow truly old."

They stopped talking. Neither of them wanted to carry on the conversation.

From the house came the sound of Armando's snoring. Sofia smiled at the thought of him. He was the man who had made love to her for the first time. And he hadn't left her, hadn't faded into the blue moonlight.

Lydia nodded off where she sat by the fire. She too snored, but woke when Rosa whimpered. Sofia got up and went into the house to breastfeed her baby. Armando slept on.

A little later, Lydia stopped in the doorway to look at her daughter feeding Rosa by candlelight.

"I'll keep living for a lot longer," she said with a smile. "You're right. I'm not old enough to die."

FOR SOFIA AND HER FAMILY this was a good time. Long afterward, Sofia believed that she had never laughed as much as during the year when her Rosa was born. Or maybe she had, when she was very young? She couldn't remember.

WHEN ROSA WAS THREE MONTHS OLD, Sofia had to go to the hospital in the city for a checkup. Rosa had to come with her, but the two older children could be left with Lydia. Armando, who had kept nagging until he was allowed to borrow one of Samuel's old cars, came to pick up Sofia and the baby. The engine smoked and rattled, its frame was bent, the windows either didn't open or couldn't be closed, but Armando held the car door open for Sofia with pride.

They drove along the road through the village, past the fields where Lydia worked, and then took the paved main road to the city.

"One day, we'll have a car of our own," Sofia said.

"How could we ever afford that?"

"Don't know. But why not?"

There were times when Sofia thought Armando was a

little too cautious. Unlike Sofia, who was quite prepared to believe that everything was possible, he often held back from making wild plans for the future. But why shouldn't they be able to afford an old car one day?

The traffic grew heavier, and exhaust fumes seeped into their car. Sofia covered Rosa's face and wondered at the crowds. How could the city hold so many people? Where did they all live? And where did they work? How did they eat? Armando drove carefully, but all the same he had to brake hard several times. Finally, they arrived.

The hospital! Sofia had been taken here after her accident and, seeing it, she felt her heart contract.

She had been unconscious for several days, but once she woke up she had been in constant, terrible pain. She shuddered at the memory.

Her sister Maria had died here. Thinking of little Rosa in her arms, Sofia was close to tears. Armando noticed that her eyes were growing shiny. He didn't ask any questions, only helped her out of the car and said he'd pick her up in the evening.

SOFIA WALKED ALONG THE HALLWAYS she knew so well. Everywhere, sick people were sitting or lying down. The air smelled of fever and dirt, of vomit and fear.

Sofia knew from her own experience that fear has a smell.

She arrived at the department for people who had lost limbs. This was where she had been fitted with artificial legs and learned to walk again with the help of crutches.

Suddenly she heard her name called by someone coming through a door, a young woman of her own age in a nurse's uniform. Sofia recognized her face, but couldn't place her.

The nurse came closer.

"Don't you recognize me?"

In that instant, Sofia knew who it was. To make sure, she glanced at the nurse's legs. She was right! The nurse had one artificial leg.

It was Hortensia, the girl from a faraway village who had also stepped on a landmine. They had become friends during the bad days in the hospital. Then, one day, Hortensia had left to go back home and they hadn't seen each other since. Not until now, ten years later.

"Hortensia! After all this time!"

"I've dreamed about you," Hortensia said. "And now we're both standing here face to face. And you're holding a baby in your arms."

They sat down on a seat in the hallway, looking at the baby and at each other.

"It's been ten years," Sofia said. "I was so sad when you left."

"Me too...but happy as well, because I was going home."

Hortensia told the story of how she had trained to become a nurse, despite her artificial leg. At first, she had needed a crutch, later just a stick, and then, finally, nothing at all.

"Are you married?" Sofia asked. "Do you have any children?"

"I'm not married yet. But I do have a boyfriend. He works here at the hospital. He's a carpenter."

Sofia told the story of her own life, about the children and Armando. And about going to school and how she too had dreamed of becoming a nurse, or even a doctor.

"I envy you," she said. "I'm so pleased to see you in a white uniform. But I wish I could be you."

"Of course you can become a nurse."

"No, I can't. I'll never be able to walk without some kind of support. And that won't do for nursing."

Hortensia didn't say anything, because she knew that Sofia was right.

"I'm here to get my final pair of artificial legs," Sofia said after a while. "I've stopped growing now, so I probably won't need to replace them again. The new pair should last me for the rest of my life. Unless they break, that is."

Hortensia, who had been through it herself, knew all about how you must keep replacing artificial limbs as you grow.

"You'll be pleased to hear this," she said. "Guess who's still working here?"

"The nurse called Mariza?"

"No. She's on duty in another ward now."

"I can't think who."

"Try!"

Sofia tried hard to remember, but it was so long ago and so many people had helped her.

"Doctor Raul. Is it him?"

"I haven't seen him for years. He might be working somewhere else."

"I can't guess."

"Yes, you can!"

"Give me a clue."

Hortensia's lips formed an O.

"Po-po-po," she said.

Sofia felt a nice warm glow of recognition.

"Master Emilio! It's him, isn't it?'

"Yes, it is."

"But isn't he very old?"

"Sure. Still here, though."

Of course Sofia remembered old Emilio, who had always helped her when she was sad and needed comforting. He fitted artificial limbs and muttered *po-po-po* to himself while he measured you for a new pair of legs.

Hortensia had to get back to work. She took Sofia's hand and held it.

———

"Where do you stay?" she asked.

"I should go back to the village tonight," Sofia replied.

"You can stay with me," Hortensia said. "I have a room in a house not far from here. It's on the ground floor, so you don't have to climb stairs."

"What will your boyfriend say?"

"Stefano? He won't mind. I've told him about you."

"Don't forget that I've got three children now," Sofia said. "Let me think about it."

Hortensia hurried away and Sofia watched her go. Her artificial leg was hardly noticeable. Seeing this, Sofia felt a little down. Then she reminded herself that she was alive and a mother. Gloomy thoughts were simply a waste of time.

WHEN SHE STEPPED INTO THE FITTING ROOM, Master Emilio was waiting for her. He saw the baby, waggled his head, and greeted her with a *po-po-po*.

"So, you're bringing your own child now," he said. "And you've come for your last pair of legs, if I remember right. How quickly time passes!"

"I've just met Hortensia," Sofia told him. "I haven't seen her in ten years."

"Yes, yes. Time passes. Almost unbearably slowly, when you're a child. Or not at all. Either you don't think about time, or it drags. Then it starts speeding

———

up and by the time you get to my age it's rushing past. The time you spend thinking about someone you don't believe you'll ever meet again is the worst. And when you do meet, the time since you last met seems both long and short."

Sofia wasn't sure she understood what Master Emilio meant. He could become entangled in words when he tried to express what he had on his mind.

"But look at your little one! Boy or girl?" he asked.

"A girl. She's called Rosa. I have another daughter, too. She has the same name as my sister who died when I lost my legs."

Master Emilio nodded slowly.

"I remember," he said gently. "You two were sisters. One of you died."

She felt a lump rise in her throat. By now, not many people remembered, but Maria still lived in Master Emilio's memory.

"Po-po-po. Now, let us have a look at your legs. Put your baby on my chair."

When Sofia had put the sleeping Rosa down, Master Emilio began to examine her artificial legs, which were held in place with straps around her waist.

"Time to replace these," he said. "Do they rub?"

"Not badly. But they hurt a bit if I go on a long walk."

"Then we'll do something about that. First I must measure you."

When Armando came to pick her up, it was already late in the afternoon. Sofia had been feeding Rosa while she waited for him outside the hospital. Her seat was close to where she had been sitting in a wheelchair ten years ago, without legs. Now, her new artificial legs would be ready for her in two weeks' time. Apart from repairs, they were meant to carry her for the rest of her life.

Sofia was still excited about seeing Hortensia and Master Emilio. Perhaps Doctor Raul was still around somewhere in the hospital, like Sister Mariza. So much had happened, so many encounters with people from the past. And Hortensia had offered her a place to stay in the city.

She watched the people hurrying along the street. Women carrying large packages on their heads, heavily loaded cars, ragged children everywhere. All the same, the thought of living in the city tempted her. But she couldn't bring her children here. And what would Armando say? She dismissed the whole idea and told herself that the most important thing was having met Hortensia. This time, they wouldn't let ten years pass before seeing each other again.

She jumped when a car horn sounded close by. Armando came and picked Rosa up in his arms. Sofia had so much to tell him and at first didn't give herself time to eat the corn on the cob he had brought for her.

———

Armando cautiously inched the car into the stream of traffic while Sofia talked.

"I don't understand a word you're saying," he said. "Come on. Eat first, then talk."

Sofia suddenly realized how hungry she was. She blushed at the thought of her childish eagerness to tell a story. How embarrassing to have shown Armando what a baby she could be.

When they reached the village it was evening already and she had had time to go through everything that had happened, with one exception: Hortensia's suggestion that Sofia could stay with her for a while. She wasn't sure how Armando would react and didn't want to make him angry.

Evening or not, Armando had to drive the car he had borrowed from Samuel back to the city. Three days later, it would be Saturday and he was due to come home again, as usual.

THAT NIGHT, SOFIA DREAMED about Hortensia. They were both in the hospital wearing white nurses' uniforms and neither of them had to wear their artificial legs. They were dancing together down hallways lined with sick people.

In the morning, Sofia remembered the dream and wrote it down in her diary. She tried to write at least a few lines every day.

Two weeks later, Sofia traveled to the city again to have her new legs fitted by Master Emilio. Baby Rosa came with her, tied to her back.

She sought out Hortensia and told her about the dream.

"We won't get our legs back," Hortensia said. "But now we've got each other."

Sofia strapped on her new legs. She was pleased with them. They didn't rub and made her a bit taller.

"There, that's it. You won't grow any taller now," Master Emilio said. "I hope you won't forget me. Come and see me now and then."

"I promise."

Once the new legs were fitted, Sofia had several hours to wait before Armando would pick her up. She and Hortensia went off to buy lemonade from the stall in front of the hospital. It was very hot and they were both sweating. Not that they let that stop them from talking. Afterward, when Sofia thought about it, it was obvious that she had missed having someone her own age to talk to, and especially someone who had known her as a child. Such people were rare, now that most of the village girls of her age had married and moved away.

She and Hortensia promised each other that they would stay in touch. Sofia found a piece of paper and drew a map to show how to find the village and her home.

Hortensia suddenly fell silent.

"I must tell you something that will make you sad," she said eventually.

Sofia felt a little queasy.

"It's about Doctor Raul," Hortensia went on.

"What about him?"

"He's dead."

Sofia's heart contracted. How could Doctor Raul be dead? He would still have been a young man. Tears filled her eyes.

"I had to tell you. I couldn't stand pretending any longer."

"How did he die?"

"He drowned. He was swimming on that island off the coast, the one called Inhaca. I don't know exactly how it happened. But they found his dead body on the beach."

"When was this?"

"A year ago? Maybe two. I'm not sure."

Sofia wanted to scream. Doctor Raul had helped her so much, maybe more than anyone else. It wasn't fair that he had drowned. That was as unfair as Maria's death, and Rosa's. She grabbed hold of her crutches, got up, and gestured toward the church next to the hospital.

"I want to go in there," she said. "Do you want to come?"

Hortensia went with her to the church. It turned out to be empty, apart from two elderly women doing some dusting. Sofia put a candle in a holder and lit it. They found a pew and sat together in silence. When Sofia started crying, her friend took her hand and held it.

But Hortensia had to go back to work and they parted outside the hospital. Sofia sat down to think about Doctor Raul and about sudden death.

TIME PASSED, A FEW MORE MONTHS of "the good time." When Rosa was five months old, Sofia took her to Doctor Nkeka.

"She's in good shape," he said, after examining the baby. "Does she cry much?"

"Not very."

"Anyway, she must be eating properly. Her weight is just right."

SOFIA TIED ROSA IN PLACE on her back and walked home. Black clouds were piling up on the horizon. If she didn't hurry, the rain would start before she reached the house.

That night, a thunderstorm rolled overhead. The children slept by her side, but she lay awake listening to the rumbling and counting the flashes of lighting. Later, a fresh night wind blew away the heavy heat of that day.

The next day was a Saturday. Sofia cooked a stew with a few small chunks of meat, some vegetables, and rice.

___

Then she settled down to wait for Armando.

She waited patiently, but he didn't come.

Gradually, anxiety began moving in on her, crawling under her skin as if a snake had entered her body unnoticed.

TEN O'CLOCK AT NIGHT. Still no Armando. When Lydia asked about him, Sofia tried not to seem worried. It had happened before when he had a lot to do.

They ate their evening meal. All the time, Sofia kept an eye on the dark road where Armando would come walking along after getting off the bus or the truck, if he had got a ride as far as the other riverbank.

Eleven o'clock.

"He has never been as late as this," Lydia said.

Sofia, who was becoming annoyed with her mother, didn't reply. Lydia was making a fuss about something that was none of her business. This was Sofia's problem, nobody else's.

Twice, she thought she had seen him. The first time, it turned out to be old Alfonso, who had had one beer too many. He was humming as he wandered toward his ramshackle house, where he lived by himself now that his wife had died and all his children had moved away.

"He drinks too much," Lydia said. "Same story as with Mrs. Mukulela."

"Oh, leave them be," Sofia hissed.

Lydia just looked wonderingly at her daughter, who sounded like an angry cat. Sofia flared up quickly at times, and Lydia didn't always understand the reason why.

Next time, it was the Basima brothers who appeared out of the shadows over the road.

Toro and Eduardo made a living from fishing in the river and always walked back home late at night. They waved to Sofia.

"We're hungry," Toro shouted. "Ask us in for supper!"

"All finished!" Sofia called back. "You'll get fed at home."

"How are the children?"

"They're fine."

"Where's Armando?"

"Still working."

The brothers disappeared into the dark. Lydia picked up the plates and started to do the dishes. Sofia went to check on the sleeping children.

When Sofia came outside again, Lydia was sitting near the fire. Sofia lost her temper instantly. Was it so hard to understand that she wanted to be left alone to wait for Armando?

———

Why didn't he come? She couldn't bear the thought that he might have been in an accident. Surely there'd be a simple explanation?

But Sofia wanted to be on her own while she waited for him and not have to share her anxiety with anyone else.

She sat down by the fire. Lydia said nothing. They both sat in silence. Around them, the village was very quiet. The road was empty. A night bird hooted somewhere far away.

Finally, Lydia said good night and went into the house. Sofia put more wood on the fire. Angry flames leapt and danced. Lokko came padding out of the night and rubbed his nose against her arm. Sofia patted him and then pushed him away. He settled down as usual, on the opposite side of the fire, and looked at her. Sofia looked back and stuck her tongue out. Lokko yawned and Sofia stuck her tongue out again. Lokko curled up with one paw across his nose.

Sofia waited.

Midnight.

She tried to imagine what could've made Armando so late. Sometimes Samuel was difficult and insisted that a particular car must be fixed before shutting up shop. But this late? And on a Saturday night?

An accident was of course still unthinkable. Armando would come soon, and then he'd explain.

———

IT WAS ONE O'CLOCK in the morning when he finally appeared. Sofia, who had been dozing by the fire, jerked awake when she heard his footsteps. Lokko woke as well, and ran to meet him.

Armando looked tired. His eyes were bloodshot.

"Why are you so late?" Sofia asked.

"We had lots of work all day."

"This late on a Saturday?"

"There was one car we had to finish."

"In the middle of the night?"

Sofia could hear the tension in her voice.

"That's right. In the middle of the night." Armando sounded sharp, too. "It took time and anyway, there are hardly any buses this late."

He was standing in deep shadows, but Sofia could see that he had washed his hands before leaving work. Sometimes he came home dirty, because he preferred to wash at home. Sofia would scrub his back for him.

"If you hadn't bothered to wash, you could've been home earlier," she said.

Armando didn't reply and kept out of the firelight, his face hidden in the shadows.

"I'll scrub your back for you, if you like. It won't take long to heat some water."

"It's too late. I can't start washing now."

"But you said you've been working, didn't you?"

"I washed before I left."

"You usually don't."

"But I did tonight."

Sofia felt a stab of fear. At first, she had been glad that Armando was home at last. Now, she felt uneasy. Something was wrong about him standing there, about his shadowy face and the way he spoke.

"Are you hungry?" she asked.

"I've eaten."

"What?"

"I bought some roasted corn. And two apples. I'm not hungry. Just sleepy."

THEY WENT INSIDE. Sofia lit a candle. They tiptoed so as not to disturb the children, who were sleeping on a mattress on the floor. Armando crept into bed. Sofia blew out the candle before sitting down on the edge of the bed to undress and take off her artificial legs. She was still too shy to be naked in front of Armando, despite the three children they had made together. She put on her nightgown and crawled in under the thin blanket, expecting Armando to reach out and pull her close. Then they'd make love, as they did every Saturday night, except when she was too big-bellied with one of their babies.

But this time he didn't touch her. She waited, listening to his breathing, sensing his body near hers. She put her hand on his cheek. He didn't move.

"Are you asleep?" she whispered.

He didn't answer. He slept. Sofia felt disappointed, because she always longed for their time in bed together when he came home. She turned on her side and closed her eyes. Of course, what he told her must be true; he was tired after a very hard day's work. Come to think of it, she might go to the city to tell Samuel that her man was coming home very late on Saturdays and was so exhausted he fell asleep far too soon.

THE NEXT DAY, to Sofia's relief, Armando seemed his old self. He played with the children, helped Lydia carry the firewood home, and talked for a long time with Sofia about what had happened during the week. Several times, she was on the verge of asking him why they hadn't made love last night. But she didn't. She wondered if she'd ever dare ask him about such things. Would she ever learn to be as direct as Hortensia?

Late on the Sunday night, Armando set out for the city. Sofia followed him down to the road.

"Here's where we once stood together," she said.

This seemed to puzzle him. His confusion saddened her.

"When we met for the first time, Armando. When you were standing here in the moonlight."

Now he understood what she meant.

"It was such a long time ago," he said apologetically. "But of course I remember."

He leaned down to scratch Lokko behind the ears. Then he kissed Sofia on the cheek.

"Kiss my lips," Sofia said. "Not my cheek."

He kissed her on the lips and wandered off down the road. Sofia stayed, watching him for as long as she could still make him out in the dusk.

DURING THE NEXT WEEK, Sofia gradually forgot how worried she had been about Armando's lateness. The night they didn't make love slipped from her mind, too. For one thing, she was very busy at her sewing machine. Several villagers had handed in clothes that needed alterations or mending. The sewing machine still worked well enough, old and worn as it was.

One dream that Sofia and Armando shared was that they would be able to connect to the village electricity supply. Until just a few years earlier, the idea had seemed utterly impossible. Then a man from the village, who had earned good money in the South African mines, came back and put electrical wiring in his house. It was not far away and the glow from his lamps lit up the night sky, once the fire in front of their house had died down.

One day they'd surely have saved up enough to pay for what was needed: just two poles, overhead cables, and wire for the house. Then Sofia could buy an electric sewing machine, the thing she wanted for herself more than anything else. Her work would become much easier and get done much faster, especially since her legs didn't work the treadle very well.

She worried about the day when the treadle would be too much for her. What would they do then? Without her sewing, they'd be very short of money. And in a few years' time, Leonardo should start going to school and they would need to earn even more to pay for his fees and books and uniform. Armando agreed with her. He understood very well what a difference an electric sewing machine would make to their income.

There were times when Sofia thought that their poverty was like a prison. How come so many people were much better off? Then again, many people lived in much worse conditions than they did. In their village, there were people who sometimes had to go to bed hungry.

Often, it was a journey to the city that reminded Sofia of how poor they were. She would notice large, gleaming cars in the streets, or catch glimpses of people seated in smart restaurants, where the cost of the food on the menu was crazily high. And there were young people of her age who seemed to have lots of money. She sometimes envied them. Not only did they have real legs and cash in hand, they had the right clothes, cell phones, everything. Why had no mines exploded under their feet? Given a chance, she'd have liked to steal their clothes and their money. And, if it were possible, she would have taken their legs, too...

Of course, such thoughts were shameful. But, so what? She had every right to dream about another kind of life. One day, Armando would drive a fancy car, and she would earn lots of money with her shiny new sewing machine.

She watched her children playing in the sandy yard. What would their lives be like? What could she and Armando do to help them? Poverty was their worst enemy. She decided to raise the subject with Armando next time he came home. Not that they hadn't talked about it before, but if their children were to have better lives in the future, they must keep trying to find ways out of poverty.

BY THE NEXT SATURDAY MORNING, Sofia had started to worry. Would Armando be back very late and once more fall asleep without touching her? When she called Leonardo and he didn't come at once, it annoyed her. She shook him roughly when he came running along at last. From the corner of her eye, she noticed Lydia watching her. But she didn't say anything. Neither of them did.

Then, at seven o'clock in the evening, Armando came. Lokko heard him first, as usual, and ran off into the night to meet him. Seeing him walking toward her, with the dog leaping at his legs, made Sofia feel happy, and relieved as well. Now everything would be back to normal.

Armando stepped into the light from the fire. Sofia

———

noticed his new clothes immediately. A blue shirt with a red collar, smart dress pants. Even his sandals were new. She wondered if he had bought something for her and the children. But he wasn't carrying any bags.

He was in a good mood and didn't seem tired at all.

"How do I look? Good?" he asked loudly.

"Very good," Lydia said.

He meant to ask me, Sofia thought irritably.

"You do look good," she said. "Where did you buy all that?"

"In the big market."

Sofia remembered how far the big marketplace was from Samuel's repair shop. There was no direct bus either. Did he have that much time to spare for buying clothes?

"Wasn't it expensive?" she asked.

"Not very. Besides, I needed new clothes."

And so do our children, thought Sofia. And so do I, for that matter, and Lydia and the boys. She felt tears filling her eyes and resented it. Armando mustn't notice that she was angry and upset. She wiped her eyes while Armando went off to say hello to the children and then go to the toilet.

"Very nice clothes Armando has got himself," Lydia said.

"Shut up," Sofia hissed. "It's got nothing to do with you."

Lydia looked stunned and withdrew, as always when Sofia lost her temper. She said nothing, only went back to minding the pot and cooking their evening meal.

They ate together, sitting round the fire. Armando was careful not to spill any food on his new outfit. He talked on happily, about how he had helped to repair a very, very expensive car.

"It cost 50,000 US dollars," he said.

Sofia wasn't quite sure how much one could buy with that.

"About a thousand sewing machines," Armando said. "Or electrical wiring for every house in the village."

"All that, for just one car?"

"Honestly."

"And who can afford a car like that?"

"Somebody in the government, a Minister."

"Is he a white man?"

"As black as you or me."

"And he had enough money to buy a car that expensive?" Sofia shook her head. She didn't believe it.

What made the story of the car especially unlikely was the notion that a black man could have so much money. She had always thought that the whites who had come to live in the country were the wealthiest people around. And that most white people were at least well off, while most black people were poor. Things must have changed. How, she didn't know.

"What is he a Minister of?" she asked.

"I don't know. Schools, I think."

"Schools? And he has such a lot of money? He should use his cash to build decent schools instead of buying expensive cars."

Lydia shushed her.

"Don't shout," she said. "There are always people with big ears listening in."

"I don't care," Sofia said furiously. "Leonardo will soon be starting in the village school. My old school. And it still has no windows, no doors, no desks, and no blackboards."

"Don't annoy people in power," Lydia warned. "Only bad can come of that. They'll never take any notice of people like us."

"Don't you remember how you and the other women in the village stood up to Mr. Bastardo when he wanted to sell off the vegetable fields? And you made him run away!"

"That was different."

"No, it wasn't."

Armando leapt abruptly to his feet.

"I can't stand listening to your chatter," he said angrily. "I'm going for a walk."

He turned his back on them and set out along the road.

All of a sudden, Sofia felt terrified that Armando

would never return home again. Also, her mother's words had irritated her.

"Look, you've made him angry," she said. "Why do you always have to talk on and on? It's pointless."

Sofia felt sorry when Lydia started to cry, but at that moment Rosa whimpered. Sofia went into the house, sat down on the bed, and fed the baby. All the children were settling down to sleep. When Rosa was satisfied, Sofia went outside with the baby tied to her back. Lydia had calmed down and was washing the dishes.

"Sorry. I didn't mean to get mad," Sofia said.

"Yes, you did," Lydia replied sharply. "And I don't happen to think that I talk too much."

She put down the plate she had washed and her eyes met Sofia's.

"If you and Armando have problems, it's up to you to sort things out. Don't take it out on me."

"We haven't got problems."

Lydia shrugged and kept washing the dishes.

"All's well, then," she said.

SOFIA WALKED DOWN THE ROAD, into the deep night. From somewhere out there came the sound of hymn singing. She listened. It always seemed strange to hear people's voices singing out of the darkness, a chorus among the shadows. Sofia hummed along. She wasn't a good singer, but not bad either.

———

Then she saw Armando.

"Finished fighting now?" he asked.

"Yes, Lydia is washing the dishes and the children are asleep."

They walked back toward the fire. Armando sat down on his stool and stared at his hands. Sofia watched him. And waited.

Why didn't he say anything? She could see that he was deep in thought. Usually, words poured out of him. If there was one person in the family who was a great talker, it was Armando.

Except now. He stayed silent. Sofia kept watching and waiting, but nothing happened. Lydia said good night and disappeared into the house. A little later, Armando stood up.

"I'm going to bed," he said. "I'm tired."

"I don't want you to go to sleep. I want you to hold me tight."

Sofia blushed. She had surprised herself. What had given her the courage to say that? Armando too was astonished. But he didn't comment.

Later, when she crawled in under the blanket, Armando opened his arms to hold her. For Sofia, the sensation was like floating in warm water. Now everything was well again. Armando was close to her. She hugged his body to hers and later fell asleep with her face pressed against his chest.

———

WHEN SOFIA OPENED HER EYES in the morning, Armando had already got out of bed. That was unlike him. Usually he slept in on Sunday mornings, sometimes until nine o'clock. Sofia had been up to feed Rosa in the night and Armando had been deep asleep then. She didn't wash, just put a dress on and went outside. Lydia was sweeping the yard. Lokko was lying near the ashes of the fire, chewing on a bone.

"Ma, where's Armando?"

"He's gone already. There are so many wrecked cars needing repairs that Samuel asked him to come in to work even though it's Sunday."

Sofia felt confused.

"Why didn't he wake me up? Did he leave any money?"

"He didn't want to disturb you, I suppose. And he gave me some money."

Lydia pulled out a few folded bills that she had kept inside the length of cloth she wore around her waist. One glance was enough to tell Sofia it was much less than what Armando usually gave her. She remembered his new clothes. Anger and worry began to torment her again.

"Did he say anything else?" she asked.

"He was in a hurry."

"Nothing at all?"

"What should he have said?"

Leonardo came outside. He was hungry. At the same time, Maria started to cry. Sofia felt utterly alone. As if, just now, Armando didn't exist.

THE DAY PASSED. Anxiety gnawed at her. But it was only at night, when she was sitting naked on the edge of the bed with her legs off, that a thought struck her with terrible force.

Armando was seeing another woman!

That was why he behaved so oddly. It was for that woman he had bought new clothes and left early on a Sunday morning.

The candle glowed. Sofia was very still, as if paralyzed. It mustn't be true. If Armando had met a woman he liked better than her, Sofia's whole life would fall apart.

She stayed there for a long time, holding her nightgown in her hand, too stiff to lie down.

Then she blew out the candle. Somehow, she felt safer in the dark.

"Armando," she whispered. "Come back. Don't leave me. Don't leave your children."

No answer.

Around her, the night was mute and still.

THE NEXT DAY, SOFIA DEALT WITH HER WORRIES
in her usual way: she tied Rosa to her back, left the older
children with Lydia, and walked down to the riverbank.
After beating the grass with her crutch to make sure there
were no snakes, she put Rosa down. Then she too settled
on the ground and began to talk with the dead.

This was one of her few memories of her father,
Hapakatanda, who had died when she was very young.
He had told her that you could talk with the dead as
well as the living. Her father had wanted to teach her
something important and it had stayed with her. Just
because you're dead and lie underground with grass
growing above you, it doesn't mean that you can't listen.
True, you can't speak, at least not in the ordinary way,
but somehow your answers arrive inside the brain of
the living person.

"You're my best friends," Sofia said to her sisters.
"And you know how very much I care for Armando.
I'm scared now, because I think he has found another

woman. I have no idea what to do. Why does he act like this? If he leaves me, I'll be lost. Then again, I'm not certain that I'm right. Maybe I'm just imagining that he's behaving strangely?"

She listened to their answers. They seemed to speak in one voice.

You must find out if it's true.

"But how can I do that?"

Ask him.

Sofia shook her head. She didn't dare. If she were wrong, he might become so angry he'd find himself another woman anyway.

She tuned in again.

Go to the city. Visit him, but make sure he doesn't know you're coming and doesn't see you. Then you'll find out the truth.

"Am I to spy on him?"

Maybe that's the only way, if you don't want to ask him.

Sofia realized that Maria and Rosa were right, though what they advised her seemed quite wrong.

"Where can I stay in the city?"

You know that already.

She could stay with Hortensia, of course. Take baby Rosa with her. Lydia could look after Leonardo and Maria.

Sofia patted the grass on the grave mound.

———

"You're my friends," she said. "Without you, I'd be helpless."

She pressed her cheek and ear to the ground. Inhaled the smell of the earth. Their hearts beat in mine, she thought. That's how it will be forever.

SOFIA STAYED SITTING ON THE GRAVE MOUND for a long time. Little Rosa slept, then woke because she was hungry. Sofia fed her. High above her, a plane drew curving lines on the sky. She and Armando had sometimes talked about how, just once, they'd find the money to travel in a plane. But perhaps Armando would prefer to take someone else on a flight.

Anger and dread, she wasn't sure which feeling was the stronger, made her tug at a clump of grass until it came out in her hand. For a brief moment, she felt ready to die. If Armando didn't want her and the children, she might as well lie down and die here. Join her sisters. Then she rejected the thought.

"I shall live!" she called out.

An old man carrying a basket on his head had been walking along the road, but curiosity made him stop.

"Something you want?" he asked.

"I just shouted," Sofia told him. "Because I'm angry."

The man put down his basket and wiped the sweat from his face. His basket was full of tomatoes.

"Shouting is the only thing to do when you're angry," he said. "Just plain shouting. And hope someone hears."

"I hoped that no one would hear. I hadn't noticed you."

"Well, that's another way of looking at it."

He lifted the heavy basket back on his head and walked on.

THE NEXT DAY, SOFIA TOLD LYDIA that she had to visit the hospital, something to do with the new legs. It was the first time she had mentioned an appointment to her mother, and Lydia clearly didn't believe a word of it. This was irritating, but Sofia kept quiet because she relied on her mother to look after Leonardo and Maria. Then she set out for the city with Rosa swaying on her back.

The night before, Sofia had packed a bag with a few things she needed. She had also lifted a piece of the clay floor, covering a hole where she kept a small, tin money box. No one knew about it, not even Armando. She had been saving every little bit of spare change, because there was no telling when she or Armando would suddenly be out of work. That she would use her savings to spy on Armando had never occurred to her.

It was suffocatingly hot when she started walking down the road. Armando had found a thermometer in the street once and they hung it up in the shade of the house. The temperature was extremely high, so it would be even hotter in the sun. Sofia covered Rosa's head and face, and protected her own head with a white scarf. She might have to walk all the way to the main road, where the buses were, and the trucks that took passengers.

She was in luck. Before long, a tractor pulling a trailer slowed down and the driver called her name. He offered her a ride, and helped her up on the trailer to join a few goats and chickens in cages.

"Lydia is a friend of mine," he said. "You mustn't walk in this heat."

Sofia sat down on one of the chicken coops. Even though the tractor didn't move very fast, a cool breeze blew up there. They passed orange groves and vegetable plots. Everywhere, men and women were at work with their hoes.

Sofia's luck held when they reached the main road: one of the passenger trucks had just stopped. Not only was it on its way to the city, but its run would end outside the hospital. Sofia paid and was helped up onto the back. It was crowded, but in the end she found a seat on the ledge behind the driver's cab. The other travelers were as poor as she was. Many went to the city hoping to find a job. Sofia thought that she was probably the only one who was on her way to spy on her man.

SHE CLAMBERED DOWN FROM THE TRUCK outside the hospital.

But now, her luck seemed to have run out. Hortensia had the day off and no one seemed to know where she lived. Sofia feared that she'd have to sleep outside that night. She was quite sure that the money she had brought wasn't enough to pay for a room in a hotel. Besides, she must buy food and pay for a trip back home.

She went to the ward where Master Emilio worked. He was surprised to see her.

"Sofia! Is there something wrong with your new legs?"

"No, my legs are fine. But I can't find Hortensia. And I don't know where she lives."

Master Emilio thought for a moment.

"I'm sure I don't either."

"I had hoped to stay with her. Now I don't know what to do."

"Space is tight where I live. And it's quite a long way away. Rides in buses and trucks, lots of changes."

Master Emilio fell silent.

"Po-po-po," he muttered thoughtfully.

"You can sleep here," he said in the end. "Among my extra limbs. I won't lock up. Then you can come and go. Anyway, it's better than sleeping outside and getting bitten by mosquitoes."

He found an old blanket and fixed a pillow for her

by bundling up some of his overalls. Together they spread a few straw mats in a corner of the room where arms and legs made of wood or plastic dangled from the ceiling.

"You're not afraid of the dark, are you? Scared of all these arms and legs?"

"No, I don't think so."

"I'll be in extra early tomorrow. Bring you breakfast. You go off and have something to eat now. When you're ready, just come here and close the door. The night watchmen won't disturb you."

Sofia bought herself a piece of bread, a few oranges, and a bar of chocolate. Actually, she wasn't hungry at all, but forced herself to eat. Afterward, she went to Master Emilio's workshop and closed the door. She stretched out on the mats with Rosa at her side. Above her, in the gathering dusk, the artificial limbs were dangling. She thought of the time she had been left for a whole night sitting in a wheelchair outside the hospital. So long ago now. Things happened all the time, unpredictable things. She couldn't ever have imagined that one night she'd sleep in Master Emilio's workshop.

HER SLEEP WAS RESTLESS, but when Master Emilio arrived in the morning he had to wake her.

"You must've had some sleep after all," he said. "Look what I've brought you to eat."

"Yes, I did sleep. But I was dreaming about all these limbs up there."

"They'll make many people happy. Remember what I said the first time you were here? That the legs I'd give you would become your best friends?"

"Yes, I remember. You were right, too. I used to call my right leg *Kukula* and my left one *Xitsongo*. The short one and the long one."

Master Emilio put on a lab coat and took down one of the legs.

"This one is for a boy of seventeen," he said. "He didn't step on a landmine. Sadly, he got in the way of a bad-tempered hippopotamus. All the same, he was lucky. A hippo can bite a human being in half. This boy lost his leg, but at least not his life."

Sofia shuddered at the thought. There were hippos upstream in the river that ran near her village. City people always feared the crocodiles more than the hippos. Crocs had such terrifying jaws and looked like dragons. The hippos, on the other hand, were dull, heavy bodied, and looked almost friendly. But Sofia, who lived among animals, knew that a hippo could run very fast, despite its large body, and bite hard with its huge mouth.

Master Emilio had brought her corn porridge in a tin bowl. She was hungry and ate it all. Then she changed Rosa and gave her a morning feed. Now she was ready to set out in search of Hortensia.

——

"If you don't find her, you can sleep here tonight," Master Emilio said. "Are you sure the limbs didn't spook you?"

"No. I'm not scared of ghosts."

"You're quite right. No need to fear ghosts. People, now that's different. Good reason to be afraid of them at times."

It didn't take Sofia long to find Hortensia. She heard her friend's loud laughter in a hallway. There she was, surrounded by a crowd of patients who practically fought about who was to be allowed to see the doctor first. Hortensia wasn't impatient with them and kept explaining that they had to wait their turn. The doctor could only see one person at a time. When she caught sight of Sofia, she looked surprised, waved, and pointed to a seat.

"I'll be done soon," she shouted. "I'm on police duty here every morning to make sure that people see the doctor in the proper order."

But it took almost half an hour before Hortensia sank down on the seat next to Sofia and drew a breath. Then she burst out laughing.

"It's like this every morning! Honestly, sometimes I dream that I'm wearing a police uniform. And that I'm standing at a street corner directing traffic with white gloves on my hands."

She rose, pulled Sofia along into a room full of old folders, chairs, and broken beds, and shut the door behind them.

"I didn't know you'd be back in town so soon."

Sofia felt embarrassed. In a flash she realized that she hadn't prepared what to tell Hortensia. She had no intention of lying, though.

Then Rosa started to cry. Both women tried to soothe her, but couldn't.

"She has a sore stomach sometimes."

"I can hear you anyway," Hortensia said.

Sofia kept talking, over the screaming. She wanted to explain exactly why she had come. At first, Hortensia seemed confused, but after a while she nodded now and then. As Sofia neared the end of her story, Rosa calmed down.

She cries because all this hurts her, too, Sofia thought. Could it be that children hear and understand much more than grown-ups believe? And that you forget as you grow up?

"I have to go back to work," Hortensia said. "Give me a few hours. Then I can slip away and take you to where I live."

Suddenly, Sofia started to cry. The tears were completely unexpected. She bit her lower lip and managed to stop.

"It's good for you to cry," Hortensia said. "I cry

as often as I can. Somehow, one laughs more easily afterward."

SOFIA LEFT THE HOSPITAL and went to sit on a low, stone wall near the main entrance. Everywhere, people were hurrying off in different directions.

A sudden insight told her that she couldn't get used to living in a big city, not ever. She was born in a village and that's how she wanted to live.

While Sofia was waiting, people came along to try to sell her things. They were mostly little boys, but sometimes old men or women also offered goods for sale. In her head, she drew up a list of what they were selling:

TV antennas, plastic sandals, cigarette lighters, toy tomahawks, soap, clothes hangers, shoelaces, sewing needles, door handles, bicycle pumps, sunglasses, talking toy frogs, pictures of a girl singer called Madonna, razors, flowerpots, shoehorns...

She gave up in the end. The space in her memory simply wasn't enough to keep a record of all the offers she turned down. Most of the street sellers were very poor and many looked close to starvation. Sofia felt almost ashamed that she had eaten and just sat there, saying no to everything she was offered.

Then, suddenly, the air filled with the wailing of sirens. Sofia thought it was fire trucks, but it was a squad of police on motorbikes. They halted the traffic and, moments later, a cavalcade of fast-moving black cars passed by. Soon, the sirens faded away in the distance. Sofia heard someone say that it was the President.

I've seen his car, Sofia thought. I couldn't see him, not through those dark windows. The question is—did he see me?

HORTENSIA FINALLY ARRIVED and, as always, she was in a hurry. Sofia thought maybe it was just as well that her friend had lost only one of her legs, because she was always so busy.

"Let's go," Hortensia said. "I can't be away for long. Shall I carry Rosa?"

Sofia tried to protest, but Hortensia tied the baby to her back.

"I need to practice," she laughed. "I guess I'll have a little one too sometime soon."

Sofia found it hard to keep up with Hortensia. She was just about to say that she couldn't take any more, and that they had to walk more slowly, when Hortensia stopped. They had arrived. Sofia was astonished to see a house set back inside a garden.

"Do you live in there? It's very nice," she said.

"No such luck! I stay in half a garage, round the back."

When Sofia stepped into Hortensia's home, she felt

———

grateful for her own house. The garage had been divided down the middle with a wall made from some old boards. The cement floor was covered with straw mats. The room that was Hortensia's had only one small window and smelled of oil and gas. It was furnished with a couple of beds, a table, two chairs, a hand basin, and a small gas stove.

"If you want a pee or whatever, there's a toilet in the backyard," Hortensia said. "How do you like it?"

Sofia thought it was awful, but her friend was clearly proud of the place.

"It's very nice."

"Come on. You mustn't tell lies. But you know, I'm so pleased that Stefano and I have got somewhere to stay at all. In the city, it's either something like this or somewhere far away. And then everything we earned would go to expensive bus fares."

Sofia looked around.

"Do you have enough room for me?"

"You can use that bed. We'll share the other one. Do you snore?"

"I'm not sure."

"Well, I do. Everyone snores. Anyway—you're welcome!"

Then Hortensia set out for the hospital. Sofia went to sit in the yard outside the garage, where the smell of engine oil wasn't so strong. She thought it was strange that she should be staying in a garage while she was trying to find out what Armando was up to, apart from car repairs.

Jealousy and fear gripped her again. Perhaps it was even worse now that she was so much closer to Armando.

I can't wait, she thought. I must find out if what I think is really true. But I dread it.

She walked through the city, taking her time so she wouldn't get lost. She knew the layout of the streets quite well, but all the same the possibility of making mistakes worried her. Besides, construction was going on all the time, old houses were being torn down and new ones built at a reckless speed. Hoping to break free from the grip of poverty, people moved to the city from everywhere, from Sofia's village, too.

At last! She stopped near a jacaranda tree that had just dropped its beautiful flowers, which lay like a blue carpet in front of her. From here, she could see the house with Samuel's workshop on the ground floor. Cars that had been taken apart were left on the pavement and in the yard of a ruined building. She saw people working, but didn't spot Armando anywhere.

Her heart was thumping. What would she say if he saw her?

I've come to say hello, she told herself. That's all. It's

only natural that a woman would want to see her man's place of work.

A rusty old bus without wheels had been left farther along the street. From over there, she'd have a better view of who did what at Samuel's workshop. Sofia crept along a wall until she reached the bus.

Rosa was stirring. Sofia rocked from side to side and Rosa went back to sleep. Soon she'd be hungry and wake up, but Sofia had some more time to keep an eye on what was going on.

The first thing she saw was a pair of legs that belonged to Armando. Nothing else. Legs, in dark blue work pants, and two bare feet. He was lying under a car, hammering at something. Sofia listened to the noise.

As long as he's lying under a car and not with another woman, it's fine with me, Sofia thought.

She had almost made up her mind to walk over to him, give his feet a good tug, and ask him why he had left so early on Sunday. But she stayed where she was. Then Rosa woke up. Sofia sat down on the steps of the bus and fed the baby and changed her.

She hugged Rosa close while she put her head around the corner again. Armando had got up, still holding a wrench, and stood talking to Samuel. Samuel pointed at the car, apparently explaining something. Armando crawled back under it again.

Sofia watched for what seemed a long, long time. By

late afternoon she was tired and hungry, but still not ready to give up. She was determined to stay until Armando left work, and find out what he did then.

A boy pulling a cart full of bananas came along. Sofia bought a bunch. She could afford bananas, but still worried about money. Would she have enough? Maybe Hortensia expected to be paid for letting Sofia sleep in her place? Sofia didn't think so. You surely wouldn't want friends to pay? But she didn't know for sure. The city was so different from her village.

The evening drew in, a brief twilight enveloped the city. A few street lamps cast their light on the cars. One by one, Samuel's workers set out for home. In the end, only Armando was left. He walked toward the backyard and she lost sight of him.

Sofia waited. When he returned, he had changed his clothes and his hair had been smoothed down with water. He spread a newspaper on top of a stack of old car tires before sitting down.

Now what? Sofia watched. He yawned and Sofia couldn't help herself, she too had to yawn. Rosa moved about on her back. Not now, Sofia thought. Please, not now. Sleep on, for just a few minutes more. I want to find out what happens next.

Time passed, infinitely slowly. Sofia thought of time wriggling drowsily along, like a snake on a chilly morning before the sun had warmed it.

Time is a snake and can move very fast, as well as at a crawl.

Armando didn't move. He was using a nail to clean the muck from under his nails. Now and then he'd look up and watch the people passing by. Nothing happened. He checked his hands again. Glanced down the street.

It had taken Sofia a while to realize that he was looking only in one direction. He's waiting for somebody, she thought. The anxiety returned, and a worse pain than ever before gripped her insides.

Rosa shifted about impatiently. Sofia rocked her. Rosa, keep quiet. Shut up, don't make a fuss.

Then she saw what she had tried not to believe, but had feared in her heart.

Armando rose quickly. A woman came striding along the sidewalk. Her skirt was short and her tightly braided hair showed off the shape of her head. Walk past him, Sofia thought. Don't stop.

But she stopped. Armando took her hand and leaned forward to touch her cheek with his lips. Then they walked away, into the night.

A cry went up inside Sofia. Armando was doing the forbidden thing! Curse him! Why didn't he want her anymore?

Sofia's body stiffened. The burning, twisting pain in her stomach made her feel sick. She wanted to throw up and had to sit down on the sidewalk.

She didn't know how long she sat there. She couldn't think—only saw the image of the woman with her pretty braids and long legs. And Armando, his lips, and the darkness that enclosed them both.

SHE CAME BACK TO REALITY when someone dropped a few coins in front of her. What? Did that woman think she was a street beggar?

It made her furious.

"I don't beg," she shouted.

She threw the coins after the confused woman.

Then she got up, brushed the dust off her clothes, and settled down on the steps of the bus. Rosa was hungry again. I hope my milk doesn't taste sour like lemon juice, Sofia thought. It's Armando who should taste my bitterness, not my children.

She wanted to cry, but clenched her teeth. A sense of being alone in the world overwhelmed her.

Then she started out for Hortensia's place. She knew it could be dangerous to walk the street after dark. But she wasn't afraid.

No one could hurt her more than Armando already had.

THE NEXT DAY SOFIA WENT BACK HOME.

During the night, Rosa had had a bad stomachache. Not only had Sofia been kept awake, but Hortensia and Stefano, too. Once or twice, Sofia had felt a terrible urge to suffocate the wailing baby, though she didn't, of course. Hortensia got up to help her, and Stefano plugged his ears with cotton batting and tried to sleep. The family who lived on the other side of the thin wall banged on it and shouted that they needed to sleep.

In the end, Sofia had started to cry. Oddly enough, Rosa stopped screaming soon afterward.

Sofia didn't have time to tell Hortensia everything about what had happened, what she had seen. All she said was that she had been right to fear that Armando had found someone else. Perched on a pile of tires, he had sat waiting for a woman, whose hips swayed as she walked. There was no way she could know for sure, but for some reason Sofia believed that Armando's new woman had not yet had children.

This caused her more pain than anything else. Armando was making love to a woman and might one day father her child.

"Threaten him," Hortensia had advised her.

"Threaten him? How?"

"Tell him that he has to choose between you and this woman. And that if he makes the wrong choice, you'll throw him out."

"But I want him to be with me."

"So what? If he doesn't want to, you'll never make him."

Stefano went outside when Sofia and Hortensia began to talk about Armando. It was as if he didn't want to hear about what Armando was up to.

"What would you have done in my place?" Sofia asked Hortensia when Stefano had closed the garage door behind him.

"I would've killed him."

Sofia looked shocked.

"Of course I don't really mean it," Hortensia said. "It's not like I'd choose to spend the rest of my life in prison just because he acted like an idiot. What I mean is, I'd throw him out."

"Even if you wanted to live with him?"

Hortensia shrugged.

"You can't have everything you want. Sometimes you've simply got to decide which one is the most hurtful.

Is it missing a man who has behaved badly? Doesn't the freedom to live without being jealous or frightened make up for it?"

EARLY IN THE MORNING, when Rosa's tummy had settled down, Hortensia came along for the walk to the city square where the buses left for Sofia's village.

"Why don't you stay a little longer?" Hortensia asked.

"I can't talk to him here in the city," Sofia replied. "I don't know what to say. I must think first."

"What if he doesn't come home anymore?"

"He will," Sofia said with conviction. "I know he'll come. Then I can talk to him."

"What will you tell him?"

Sofia just shook her head. She had no answer to that. She had no idea what she would say to Armando when he actually stood in front of her.

"You can always come back here," Hortensia said.

"Yes, I know," Sofia told her. "I don't have many friends. But I know you're one of them."

Hortensia waved good-bye to Sofia and Rosa, who sat crammed into the overfull bus. It was hot and smelly. Sofia worried that Rosa would have another attack of diarrhea, but it didn't happen. Sofia fell asleep and only woke when the driver shouted to her that this was the end of the run and the bus was turning back.

IT WAS LATE IN THE AFTERNOON when Sofia got home. Leonardo and Lokko ran to meet her. She felt a little jolt of happiness for the first time since she had seen Armando with the unknown woman. Even some peace of mind. That sight had knocked her down, but now she felt ready to get up again.

Lydia didn't say anything, just looked quizzical. Sofia didn't say anything either. It was none of Lydia's business. Sofia was a grown woman. This problem was for her and her children to deal with, no one else.

THE WEEK PASSED. JEALOUSY HAUNTED HER.

Sofia wrote in her diary that the nights were the worst. She kept waking up after bad dreams. In one dream, Armando was standing naked in front of her in the moonlit road, where he had stood a long time ago. He was smiling, but when Sofia wanted to hold him, a woman stepped in between them. At that moment, she awoke. The dream returned several nights in a row.

Often, she went to bed without taking off her artificial legs. She was too restless to stay in bed all night, twisting and turning. Instead she would reach for her crutches and go outside. The nights were warm and Lokko always came to meet her, wagging his tail. Sometimes she would bring a straw mat and lie down with her head against the dog's warm body. Once the glow of the fire faded, the starry sky shone clear and strong. The stars seemed to pull her toward them.

Doctor Raul had told her that the heavenly bodies she could see were actually rushing away from her at dizzying speeds. "The universe is like an arrow," he had said. "It is flying away from us so fast we can't grasp that it is moving. One day, the starlight will disappear and everything will become black. But by then we'll be long gone."

Tears came to her eyes when she thought of Doctor Raul, of his dying alone at sea. Soon there'll be nobody left for me, she thought. Why can't Armando understand that he has to stay with me?

The very worst thing about her sleepless nights was the jealousy. It was like having swallowed a pile of ants: the ants were biting and tearing at her insides and she could do nothing to stop them. Sofia tried not to think about Armando with that woman, but she always saw them naked together and the picture wouldn't go away, not even when it made her feel so awful she'd hit her forehead with her fists.

Sometimes, she thought that Armando didn't understand what he was doing. If only she could explain, everything would be good, as it had been.

DURING THE NIGHTS AND DAYS of waiting for Armando's return on the Saturday, she carried on an argument with him in her head. At times, especially when she had worked herself up into a rage, she might start talking out loud to herself. Lydia heard her, but didn't say anything. Leonardo didn't either. Sofia carried on her imaginary talks with Armando, trying to plan not only what she would say, but what he was likely to reply.

When Saturday came at last, she took a bath in the big tub behind the curtain of yellow straw matting. Afterward, she put on her best clothes, a white blouse and a red skirt she had made the year before. She tried to be completely calm, but realized she was so nervous she was trembling all over.

Armando arrived at his usual time, just after seven o'clock in the evening. He wore his new clothes, but said he was dirty and needed a wash. He wanted Sofia to scrub his back and she said yes. When she first saw his naked back she felt like scratching it. Instead she scrubbed away, as hard as she could. She wanted to rub away every trace of that woman, whose hand he had held and with whom he had surely done forbidden things.

"Hey, it hurts," he said suddenly. "You're too rough."

"I didn't mean to be," Sofia replied. "Anyway, I'm done now."

He got up to dry himself. She turned away and busied herself with cleaning the tub and letting the water out. If she had been strong enough, she might've tipped the dirty water over him and told him that he should get his new girlfriend to wash him. But she said nothing. Only waited.

When they ate an evening meal of fried chicken, rice, and salad, everything seemed so normal. Armando talked about the past week, about the cars he had repaired. Sofia suddenly found herself wondering if she had just had a bad dream. But it was no dream. She really had been in the city and seen him wait for the woman in the short skirt.

After supper, Armando played with Leonardo and Maria and then sat holding Rosa in his lap until she fell asleep. Lydia went off to bed early that night. Sofia understood that her mother had decided to give her and Armando time alone together. She doesn't know what's wrong, Sofia thought. But she guesses that something is going on. Is that how it will be for me, too, when my children have grown up? I'll guess, but never know if or why one of them is troubled?

Armando was sitting by the fire. He threw sticks for Lokko to fetch. Sofia sat on the other side, watching them play. Dog, stick, dog, stick…

Sofia observed Armando's face through the dance of the flames. What was he thinking? Was he with her, or was his mind with the other woman? He was here, at their fire, playing a stick game with Lokko. But in his mind he might be naked in bed with that woman.

Suddenly, Sofia leaned forward and blew hard on

the fire. The flames spat and a few sparks flew toward Armando.

"What are you doing?"

"Nothing," Sofia said. "And what are you doing?"

"I'm playing with the dog. Isn't that obvious?"

It was too late to stop now. Sofia felt she couldn't bear it anymore. She *had* to know.

"Didn't you have a lot to do tonight?"

"Samuel let me off earlier than the others."

"What a shame."

"Why? It meant I got home earlier."

"But you could've stayed behind, couldn't you?"

"What are you talking about? I wanted to get home."

"You didn't want to come home two Saturdays ago."

"Have you forgotten what I said? I had to stay late because there was a lot of work to finish."

"What do you do in the evenings?"

Sofia hadn't planned to ask him this. The question leapt from her mouth, the way a caged bird leaps out when it spots that the cage door is left open. She was too late to catch the words before they took off.

"Sleep," Armando said.

He sounds like his old self, Sofia thought quickly. He isn't nervous at all. It's almost as if he had expected me to ask him that.

———

"Do you sleep in that attic room in the house on the street that runs close to the steep riverbank? The room where I came to see you once?"

"Where else? Why ask?"

"Oh, I just wanted to know."

"Wanted to know what you know already?"

This was pointless. He slipped out of her reach every time. Sofia realized that he was on guard now. It reminded her of the Saturday two weeks earlier, when he had come home late and stayed in the shadows where his face was nearly invisible. He was doing it again. Sitting on the ground, he was still edging away until his face was at least partly shadowed.

"You're not telling the truth," Sofia said, and her voice shook. "You're lying to me."

"What do you mean?"

His voice shook, too. It cracked, became high-pitched, almost a shriek.

"What I mean is that a woman comes to meet you after work. And you take her hand and then you walk away together."

Astonished, Armando stared at Sofia.

"I've no idea what you're talking about."

"Don't lie!" Sofia screamed.

By now she was furious—terrified and jealous and raging. She felt like throwing one of her crutches at him.

"I'm not lying. I don't get it. What do you mean?"

"You want to know what I mean? I'm just telling you what I saw with my own eyes. I was behind that rusty old bus without wheels. I *saw* you! Maybe you feel you're missing out because I can't wear short skirts? Because my legs look ugly? Is that it?"

She struck at him with one crutch, hitting out through the fire. The sparks flew.

"It's a mistake. What you say isn't true…it isn't what you think!"

By now Armando's voice had risen to a scream, just like Sofia's. She sensed that Mrs. Mukulela had sneaked outside to listen, standing in the shadows near her house. Sofia didn't give a damn. All she wanted was to force Armando to tell her the truth.

"I trust my own eyes. That's all."

"Have you been spying on me?"

"I didn't want to. But I had to."

"It's nothing."

"What? How can it be nothing?"

"It's finished. It's over."

"Who is she?"

"Does it matter?"

"It matters to me."

"Listen to me, I'm telling you it's nothing. And it was never serious."

"So, why did you walk off holding hands?"

"You must've made a mistake."

"No mistake, I saw it."

"I don't want to talk about it anymore. It's finished, like I said. Over and done with."

"It can't be over if it was nothing. What's her name?"

"Eliza."

"I want you to tell me what you've been doing. Now."

"Nothing."

"Can't you stop lying for once?"

"I held her hand a couple of times. That's all."

"What else did you do together?"

"Nothing."

"Did you sleep with her?"

"No."

"You expect me to believe that?"

"Yes."

"You're lying."

"I swear. Honestly, it was nothing. And now it's over."

"How did you meet?"

"What's the point?"

"I care. I want to know."

"Just, you know, like that. In the street."

"What does she do?"

"I don't know."

"You walk around hand in hand with someone you know nothing about? You don't know what she does? Maybe she's one of the girls who sell themselves in the street. Is she?"

"You're crazy."

"I want to know the truth."

"We met buying tomatoes at the same stall. We got talking. I held her hand once or twice, whatever. That's all."

Before Sofia could ask any more questions, Armando moved to her side of the fire and sat down beside her. He took her hand. She tried to pull it back, but he held it tightly, wouldn't let go.

"I didn't mean to," he said. "It isn't always easy to be on your own in the city. But what you saw was all there was. And now it's over."

"How am I to know if I can trust you?"

"By looking into my eyes."

Their eyes met.

But could she believe him? She wanted to, but didn't know if she could risk it. What would happen if she trusted him and he had been lying after all?

"Let's go to bed now," he said. "I miss you every single day in the city."

Sofia didn't reply. They sat in silence. After a while he stopped holding her hand and said he wanted to go to bed.

———

SOFIA LET THE FIRE DIE DOWN. She heard him moving about inside the house, then the bed creaking. Most of all she wanted to get up right away, skip along on her crutches as fast as she could, take her clothes off, and get into bed with him. But she stayed where she was. She needed to think. Was his explanation the truth? Had Sofia seen all there was to see?

In the end, and no wiser, she kicked sand on top of the last glowing embers and went inside. She sensed that he was awake and waiting for her. When she got into bed, he put his arm around her and tried to turn her toward him.

"Not tonight," Sofia said. "Leave me alone. You go to sleep."

He said nothing, but let his arm rest on her body.

She lay awake until she could hear that he was asleep. Her thoughts kept going in circles. But just before she went to sleep she made up her mind. She would trust him. All he and that Eliza had done was hold hands and walk through the city. Nothing more serious. He wouldn't lie to Sofia. She was the mother of his children.

BY SUNDAY NIGHT, when Armando left to go back to the city, Sofia had convinced herself that he had told her the truth. If he lied all the time, how could he act normally with his family? Sofia couldn't get her head around this and, because she couldn't, she had to believe him.

She came with him for part of the way. Sofia always liked walking on that road with Armando. Here I am, walking with my man, she told herself. People thought I'd never get anyone, because I have artificial legs. No one would want to share my bed, and sleep with a woman without real legs. But they were wrong. Armando isn't just anybody. He has a job in the city, and when he comes home on Saturdays he brings money from his wages.

That morning, Armando had handed over the amount of money she expected. Everything was back to normal now. Sofia felt hugely relieved that the whole thing had been nothing more than a nightmare after all. From now on she must trust him and forget all about the city woman.

Before they separated, he stroked her cheek lightly with his fingertips.

"I'll be back this Saturday, as usual," he said.

"And I'll be here," she replied. "I'm always here."

Lokko ran along after him until Sofia made the dog come with her.

"It's going to rain," Sofia shouted to his departing back. "If you don't hurry you'll be soaked."

He waved, then walked faster along the road.

THE NIGHT BROUGHT A WILD RAINSTORM. Sofia lay awake listening to the booming noise of rain hitting the tin roof. When it rained it was as if she lived inside a giant's drum. The rain was making its music above her head.

It made her wonder. Who dances to the sound of rain? If the rain plays the drums, surely someone must dance?

In the morning, the rain had stopped. The sandy yard in front of the house had become one large, soggy patch of mud. Lokko stood under the roof that sheltered the cooking area. His ears lay flat along his head and his tail drooped.

Sofia burst out laughing. What did she care about that soggy stuff? Now she didn't have to lie awake at night, tormented by worry and jealousy.

All that was in the past and only a sense of envy lingered because that Eliza woman could show off her legs in a short skirt. But soon she'd fade out of mind, the memory of her trampled into the muddy ground.

Later that day, Sofia had an idea. She would sew a new shirt for Armando, a surprise present. In one of the boxes behind the sewing machine was a length of material that she had saved for a long time. She knew his measurements, of course, and that evening she started to cut out the pieces and sew them together. The shirt would have a shiny, white band across the chest. It would be made just for Armando and be unlike any of the shirts one could pick up in the market.

She also made up her mind to travel to the city and

give it to him, rather than hang on to the gift until next Saturday. It was an uncomfortable trip with several changes, but Sofia felt it was worth it.

Lydia said yes at once when Sofia asked her to look after Leonardo and Maria on the day she went to the city. She obviously realizes how important it is for me to go there, Sofia thought. She sees right through me.

Two days later, the shirt was ready. Sofia woke extra early and was ready to set out by sunrise. Lydia wanted to know when she was coming back.

Sofia had an idea that she would stay the night with Armando.

"I might be back tonight. But tomorrow morning would be better."

"You stay until tomorrow," Lydia said. "It's the best way."

She understands far too much, Sofia thought again. I wouldn't be surprised if she knows what I dream about at night.

Sofia arrived in the city late in the afternoon, despite starting her travels so early. Twice, different buses had broken down, and an accident meant that her truck became stuck in traffic. When she finally arrived, she was nearly fainting with hunger. She had to eat before walking to Samuel's shop. She bought nuts and apples,

———

then asked for a glass of water in a café. It was getting dark when she set out for the workshop.

The shirt was in a cloth bag that hung around her neck. Suddenly, someone tugged hard at the bag. Sofia almost lost her balance, but managed to cling to one of her crutches. A young man of her own age had tried to rip the bag off her. Thief, she thought instantly, and it made her determined not to lose Armando's shirt. Shouting at him to stop it, she struck him on the head with her other crutch. Sheer astonishment made him let go. She kept hitting at him until he ran away.

It had been very quick. People in the street had barely noticed, but Sofia was so upset she had to lean against a wall to catch her breath. Thank goodness, Rosa hadn't even woken up. The would-be thief had been dirty and wore ragged clothes. He's poor, she thought, poorer than I am. So, the poor steal from the poor. And if one of his victims catches the thief, may God have mercy on him. She knew that the poor often have to do their own police work, and can inflict terrible punishments.

She felt frightened now. It was a bad idea to walk alone on city streets after dark, especially if you carry something like her bag.

When she arrived at the car repair shop, the workers were already sorting out their tools and getting ready to change out of their work clothes. She caught sight of Armando and was about to call out to him when something made her stop. Why had she clapped her hand to her mouth? Was it to watch Armando in the same way as Lydia watched her? To find out what was going on inside his head?

She stepped back a little and then hurried across the street to hide behind the old bus. She still couldn't understand herself. Surely she had come all this way to surprise him with the new shirt she had made for him? But instead, here she was, hiding from him again.

Once Samuel had kick-started his scooter and driven away, Armando was the last one left. She was just about to come out of hiding when she saw her. His other woman. Today she wore a different skirt, a white one, but her braided hairstyle was the same. Sofia shut her eyes tight and then opened them to look again. It wasn't her imagination, it was true.

Armando went toward the woman called Eliza. They kissed. Sofia felt a scream start deep inside her body, but she didn't let it out.

What she saw couldn't be real. And yet, it was. Armando had lied to her. Whatever they did together was not over. Nothing had finished.

They started walking. This time Sofia followed them, her eyes brimming with tears. She was jealous, she was fearful, she was everything you are when nothing seems right. I'm following him like a dog, she thought. Like a miserable dog that wants to find out why the master treats it the way he does. A couple of times she wanted to stop and run away, but she stayed on their trail. When they slowed down and kissed, she had to shut her eyes.

They stopped outside a small house, squeezed into a gap between two tall buildings. Eliza unlocked the door. When the door closed behind the two of them, it seemed to slam into Sofia's face. It felt as if the blow had drawn blood, but her face didn't bleed, couldn't respond.

Sofia pulled the bag from around her neck. Next to her, a drain with a broken grate was set into the street. She shoved Armando's shirt down the evil-smelling hole. The cloth bag went the same way. At that moment, her mind was empty of everything except hatred. She hated Armando and she hated that woman. She hated herself, too, because she had trusted him.

People who do that to me don't deserve to live, she thought as she crossed the street.

There was a light in one of the windows. She went closer and tried to look in. She couldn't see anything through the curtain, but heard voices. A woman laughed. Then, suddenly, Armando's voice. He laughed, too.

I'll kill you, Sofia thought. I won't wait. I'll do it now.

Someone had dropped a torn newspaper on the street. Nearby, a half-asleep cigarette seller had spread his merchandise out in front of him. Sofia bought a box of matches, then bent to pick up a loose rock. Her idea

---

was to break the window with the rock, and throw the burning newspaper into the house. She'd stay behind to watch. If she too burned, it wouldn't matter.

She rolled the newspaper up tightly, put the match to it, and waited until it flared up. Now she stood ready to throw the rock.

IN THAT INSTANT, she realized what she was about to do: set fire to a house, maybe kill people.

She let the rock drop and stepped on the burning paper to put out the flame.

Then she walked away. That night she slept outside, hiding in a park. Sometimes, she felt the touch of the large rats sniffing at her body. When dawn broke, she set out to catch the first bus back home.

She knew that now she no longer had a man in her life. Armando had left her. She had lost her Moon Boy.

This was the end.

—

WHEN SOFIA GOT BACK HOME, she told her mother everything.

Lydia had realized at once how sad Sofia was and taken the children to Mrs. Mukulela, who promised to keep an eye on them.

Then the whole story came pouring out. Lydia listened quietly, sitting close to her daughter on a straw mat in the shade of the house. Sofia sniffled and hiccupped, burst into tears, and wept like a child. In the end she had told how she had even been about to throw a burning torch into the house.

This upset Lydia.

"But there might've been children in the house. What could you have been thinking?"

"I didn't throw it. But I wasn't thinking then, not clearly anyway. I didn't know what to do. Still don't."

AFTERWARD, SOFIA WOULD REFLECT on how unprepared she had been for Lydia's reaction. She had felt certain that Lydia would be as furious with Armando as she was herself. Instead, Lydia responded with words that held no anger.

"What are you going to do?" was all she asked at first.

"What am I going to do? I'll throw him out. I'll bag all his clothes and leave them outside. He won't ever set foot in my house again."

"This is *our* house," Lydia said. "You might not let him into your house, but I'll let him into mine."

"What do you mean?"

"What I mean is this: you must calm down."

Sofia looked wonderingly at her mother. Lydia seemed weary, but unsurprised at Sofia's story.

"Ma, I will calm down, but not until I've packed his things away and put the bags outside."

"And how will you manage without a man?"

"I managed before he came into my life, didn't I?"

"You didn't have three children then."

"I'll be fine. But I can't live with a man who goes out with other women."

Lydia was silent for a while.

"Look, it needn't be such a terrible thing," she said hesitantly.

"What?"

"I'm sure he'll come back to you. His children are here. He lives here. He'll forget that woman."

"But I won't forget her. He lied to me. Can't you hear what I tell you?"

"Don't shout. I hear you all right."

"What would you have done if it happened to you?"

"I can answer that," Lydia said firmly. "At first, I would've reacted just like you. Cried with rage and jealousy. But when he came back I would have kept a straight face and forgiven him. Why would I? Because it makes my life easier if he is around, working, bringing money in. We're poor. It means that we can't do just what we like."

Sofia tried to break into the flow of words, but Lydia held up her hand.

"I'm not finished yet. You never really knew your father, but I can tell you that Hapakatanda behaved just like Armando. Twice, I found him running around after another woman. But I forgave him. And I never regretted it."

"My father?" Sofia said.

"That's right. Your dad. He could be very difficult. I was often angry with him. But he was the father of my children and when he was working, he helped me support the family."

"I don't care," Sofia said stubbornly. "I'm going to kick Armando out."

"You can't do that."

"Why not?"

"He can complain to the village chief. They are both men, and men make the decisions."

"They decide for you maybe. But not for me."

Lydia shook her head.

"I wish you'd listen to me," she said. "Jealousy and anger don't last. Armando will always be the father of your children."

"I won't have anything more to do with him. It's as simple as that."

LYDIA WAITED, still sitting on the straw mat. Soon Armando's clothes came flying out through the open door. She looked on for a while, then started to pick up the clothes and carry them back indoors. Sofia threw them out again. Mrs. Mukulela stood outside her house with the children in tow, watching this performance.

"What's that they're doing?" Leonardo asked wonderingly.

"I have no idea," Mrs. Mukulela said.

"Why is Mom throwing Dad's clothes into the yard?"

"You be quiet. Questions, questions. Off you go and play!"

Leonardo did as he was told.

But Mrs. Mukulela stayed where she was, looking on as Lydia and Sofia almost came to blows over Armando's clothes.

Sofia won in the end. Lydia gave in.

"Sofia, you're a fool," she screamed and flung a pair of Armando's shoes in the sand. "He'll never forgive you. He'll try to take the house from you and your little ones. And he'll complain to the village chief and he'll make his own family blame us."

"I won't have him in the house," Sofia said.

SOFIA CALLED LOKKO and they walked together to the shop on the main road. It was a rickety shed, covered with a rusty, tin roof, where Mrs. Basima sold all sorts of things. No one could understand how all that stuff could be stored away inside such a small building. It didn't help that Mrs. Basima was enormously fat. She waddled about like a duck, her face pouring with sweat. But, for all her sighing and puffing, she was always cheerful.

"Well now, Sofia Alface Fumo!" she said and laughed. "I hear you've had another baby, right?"

"She's called Rosa," Sofia said. "And she's doing very well."

"And how is Ma Lydia?"

"Well."

"And your little brothers?"

"Well, too."

"And Leonardo?"

"Just fine."

"And Maria?"

"Fine."

Mrs. Basima's memory was excellent. She knew everyone in the village, and remembered all five hundred or so individuals by name.

Now she fixed her eyes on Sofia and worried furrows appeared on her forehead.

"But you don't feel all that well, do you, Sofia?"

"There's nothing wrong with me."

"Never tell Mrs. Basima a lie. If I say you're not feeling so well, that's how it is. Am I not right?"

"Perhaps you are. But I don't want to talk about it."

"That's different," Mrs. Basima conceded. "What can I get for you?"

"Two plastic bags. Big, black ones, if you have them."

"Let me see."

Mrs. Basima bent over to look. Her fat bottom went up in the air and was all that showed over the counter. Sofia couldn't help laughing.

"What's that you're laughing at?" Mrs. Basima shouted from somewhere at floor level, in between groaning and puffing with the effort of finding the plastic bags.

"Nothing special," Sofia said. "I'm just laughing."

Mrs. Basima straightened up. Triumphantly, she produced a roll of black garbage bags.

"I knew there were some around. How many do you want?"

"Two, please."

"Tidying up, are you?"

"That's right."

Sofia could see that Mrs. Basima didn't believe her. She paid for the bags and left.

Lokko padded along at her side.

"She talks too much," Sofia said to him. "Mrs. Basima is a real village gossip. But what kind of story can she dream up about me and the bags? Maybe that I've killed somebody and carved up the corpse and now I'm going to bury the bits?"

Lokko was more interested in the different smells along the road, but wagged his tail to show that he agreed.

SOFIA SPENT THE REST OF THAT DAY packing Armando's things. As she folded the clothes, she was reminded of how many of them she had sewn for him. It was as if she were packing away their whole life together. She couldn't help crying.

Suddenly, Leonardo appeared in the doorway. She hadn't heard him come. Leonardo, like Sofia when she was little, could move about without making a sound. Wide-eyed, he observed his mother and what she was doing.

"Go outside," Sofia told him. "Don't just stand there!"

Leonardo stood absolutely still.

"Off you go!"

Sofia had raised her voice and he ran away. At once, she regretted being so harsh. Soon she would have to explain to him that she had thrown his father out of their home. But she didn't want him to watch her just now.

When she had finished, she sat down on the edge of the bed and stared at the two bags. Then she started looking through one of her old diaries until she found the time when Rosa was dying. It was also the time when she first met Armando and when she had had a strange dream about herself. Now, as she read, it came back to her:

The moonlight glowed.

Its blue flame seemed to reach down from the dark sky to her face. Then she could see herself standing in the road. The entire road was blue. She stooped and picked up a handful of sand. Grains of blue sand slid between her fingers. The sand felt warm. A blue sensation flowed through her body.

Sofia turned the pages and found the place where she had described her first encounter with Armando. At the time, she didn't know his name but called him Moon Boy.

He came walking along the road. He was smiling. When he stopped, I could smell the scent of cinnamon. Suddenly, he started taking his clothes off. He began with his shirt and gave it to me. Its collar was worn and frayed. I took the shirt and promised to mend it.

That shirt was lying on top in one of the bags. She had folded it more carefully than the other things. When she stood holding it, she had been thinking that she couldn't bear living alone, without Armando. Couldn't she put up with him meeting a woman in the city now and then, as Lydia advised? As long as Sofia was the one he came home to?

But she couldn't. That he had lied to her was harder to take than anything else.

There was a photograph in the diary. One of Mrs. Mukulela's relatives lived in the city and sometimes came to visit her. Once, he had brought a camera that developed the pictures there and then. He had taken a photograph of Armando and Sofia: they stood in front of their house, laughing and looking straight into the camera's eye.

Sofia tried to remember what she had felt back then. At peace, she thought, at last. After the terrible years of losing so much, I could laugh again. Armando didn't mind about my legs and my scarred body. He touched me, despite all that.

She examined the photograph. It seemed so incredibly long ago.

Then the image of her smiling face seemed to fade away until the picture only showed Armando laughing.

In the end, he didn't face the camera anymore, but had turned to look at a woman who was standing behind the photographer, waving a handkerchief.

Sofia put the diary away. She tied the bags and hauled them into a corner. She didn't want to leave them in the yard now. Better wait until Saturday, or rats and stray dogs might get at them.

Lydia appeared suddenly. She, too, could move soundlessly at times. She glanced at the bags, but said nothing.

"Ready to eat?" she asked. "The children are hungry."

"I don't want anything."

"Are you sick?"

"No. Not hungry, that's all."

Lydia didn't ask any more questions.

Sofia watched from the doorway while her mother filled the plates with cornmeal porridge, first for the little children, then for the boys, and, last of all, for herself.

Rosa, who had been asleep on the bed while Sofia packed Armando's clothes, woke with a little cry. Sofia picked her up and wondered if babies dreamed. Or perhaps you had to be older before dreams could take shape inside your sleeping head?

"Did you dream?" she whispered. "Was it a scary dream?"

Rosa poked her mother's face with her tiny fingers apart, so her hand looked like a starfish. Sofia sat down on the bed and put her baby to her breast. It calmed her. Even if Armando didn't care anymore, Rosa needed her.

After a while, she got up and went out into the yard. She carried on feeding Rosa. Leonardo was scraping his plate clean.

"Lydia, please give him my porridge," she said. "He's still hungry."

"I never saw a child eat like he does."

"Leonardo wants so many things. He needs food to keep going."

She sat down on a stool and rocked Rosa in her arms.

I have good children, Sofia thought. They hardly ever cry.

"What was I like when I was little?" Sofia asked Lydia, who was busy piling up the dishes. "Did I cry a lot?"

Lydia didn't reply at once. She has had so many children, Sofia thought. When I'm as old as Lydia, will I remember things like that?

"Maria cried often," Lydia said slowly. "You didn't. But you were a restless sleeper. Tossing and turning, as if you had nightmares all the time."

"And Rosa, what about her?"

"She was a dreadful one for screaming. But she had a sore stomach a lot of the time."

Lydia put their plates and cutlery in a basin. It was the same basin they used for washing.

———

"On Saturday, I'll be away from here in the afternoon," Sofia said. "Before I leave, I'll put Armando's things in the yard. I don't want to see him."

"What am I supposed to tell him?"

"I haven't made up my mind. I might write him a letter."

"You know Armando isn't a good reader."

"I'll write so he understands."

Lydia stopped washing the plate she was holding.

"Sofia, are you sure you know what you're doing?"

"No, I'm not. I'm not sure about anything. But I believe that what I'm doing is right."

"You'll regret it."

Sofia was outraged.

"You're my mother! You should back me! Not Armando, who behaved like a pig. He's a cheat! And that's all there's to it."

"Don't shout like that," Lydia pleaded.

"I'll shout as much as I like!"

"You mustn't think that I want anything but the best for you."

"Prove it!"

Sofia got up and carried Rosa into the house. Leonardo and Maria sat on the bed and looked anxiously at Sofia when she came into the room.

"Why were you shouting?" Leonardo asked.

"Because I was angry," Sofia replied. "But I'm not

angry anymore. Now you must take your clothes off, and wash, and brush your teeth. And then I'll tell you a bedtime story."

SOFIA LIT A CANDLE and crawled into bed with her children. They liked going to sleep in her bed. At her own bedtime, she'd lift them down onto the mattress on the floor. A great tenderness filled her when she saw their two little faces looking expectantly up at her.

Sofia always invented her own stories, which seemed to flow from somewhere inside her. She never planned ahead. It was, she thought at times, as if an invisible spirit wafted stories about and made them fly toward her. It was childish of course, but then, the people she liked best had a childish streak.

That evening, she told a story about a magic straw hat that would come whirling along in the wind. It could talk and tell stories about all the heads it had protected in the thousand years it had existed...

When both children were asleep, Sofia blew out the candle and went outside. She could hear the noises made by her mother and the boys as they got ready for bed in the other room. She called Lokko and set out along the road. The starry sky was very clear and the air was warm. Soon, the rainy season was due, with its hot, humid days, rain, and thunderstorms.

And *mosquitoes*.

Sofia told herself that she must buy a new mosquito net, because the one they had was torn. More than anything else, she feared that one of her children might catch malaria. One of her brothers had died from malaria. Sofia didn't want to have to face that experience ever again.

Suddenly, Lokko started growling and the fur on his back bristled. He rarely growled. Sofia stared into the night but couldn't figure out what smell had reached Lokko's sensitive nose.

Something moved. The next instant, Sofia looked into a pair of gleaming yellow eyes. A cat, she thought. No, it was too big to be a cat. Lokko's growling grew louder. His fur stood up straight now, like rows of nails.

The animal moved again in the darkness and, for a split second, she saw its body and its yellowy, black-spotted fur. She screamed.

A leopard!

It was in the village. Leopards came this close only rarely, and she had never seen one before. They killed goats and dogs.

Hurrying back to the house, Sofia stumbled and fell. Lokko barked. Other dogs joined until the whole village was filled with a chorus of barking.

Lydia had come outside to find out what was going on.

"A leopard," Sofia said. "I saw it."

At once, Lydia threw twigs and branches on the fire

and blew on the embers. Wild animals keep away from fires.

They heard Mrs. Mukulela call out.

"Why are all the dogs barking?"

"Sofia saw a leopard!"

"God help us all! Where?"

"It's gone now."

Mrs. Mukulela ran back inside and they heard her barring her door.

Sofia patted the restless Lokko to calm him. Slowly, the dogs fell silent.

The next day, as the village woke, someone might find a goat or two missing. Only the torn skins and a few bloody paw marks would be left.

THAT NIGHT, SOFIA LAY AWAKE for a long time, listening into the dark. The leopard might be prowling nearby, perhaps close to her face. She shivered. Life was always so unsafe, so insecure. Sometimes wild animals are the predators, sometimes people.

Armando had turned into a predator.

He had chased her away and picked another woman to join his pack. But when he enters this house, not a hair stands up on Lokko's back. He doesn't even growl.

ON SATURDAY MORNING, Sofia got up early. It had rained during the night, but the strong sunshine was

———

drying the ground quickly. She dragged the bags outside and handed Lydia a letter for Armando. It was just a folded note, without an envelope. Lydia found reading hard, even simple words.

"Give this to Armando, Ma. If he asks where I am, tell him you don't know. Except that I won't be back as long as he stays here."

"He'll be furious."

"He won't be angry with you. Only with me."

"But if you aren't here, he'll be mad at me instead!"

"You can always leave, too," Sofia said. "Look, I could put the letter here instead, on top of this bag. Or I could ask Leonardo to give it to his dad."

Lydia reluctantly took the letter.

"Are you really sure about what you're doing?"

"No. I'm far too young to be sure of anything," Sofia said. "But I must do what I think is right."

THAT AFTERNOON, SOFIA WALKED AWAY. She stopped at Mrs. Basima's to buy some bread and a bunch of bananas. When Mrs. Basima asked where she was off to, Sofia said she was going to Rosa's grave.

"Everybody dies and that's a fact," Mrs. Basima said. "And I will die one day, too."

She sighed heavily and shook her head.

SOFIA SAT ON THE RIVERBANK until dusk. She didn't dare stay there after dark. No one knew if the leopard would come back. The evening when she had glimpsed it in the dark, it had taken a goat. Leopards often returned to where they knew the hunting was good.

Sofia walked to Hussein's shop. She bought a cup of tea. Lots of young people came there for the beer and many had already drunk far too much. Her sister Rosa had liked going to Hussein's to dance. Sofia sat down in a corner, listened to the thumping, noisy music, and watched.

She couldn't dance anymore, and she'd never get over it. She had lost so much when the landmine explosion tore off her legs, but what she missed most was the ability to dance. She could put up with her crutches and artificial legs. But the dance! That she would never get back.

She checked her watch. By now, Armando would be at the house, unless he had been delayed again. She tried to imagine how he would react, but it was hopeless. She was certain of only one thing: he would never have expected to find his clothes packed away and Sofia gone.

She thought about her message for Armando, word for word.

Armando
I have packed up your clothes and shoes and your broken harmonica. It is all in the two bags. You cannot stay here any longer, because you do not want to live with me. You have found another woman. Stay away

for a month. Then you may come back one Sunday so we can talk about how and when you will see your children in the future.

    Sofia Alface Fumo

IT LOOKED MORE SERIOUS to have signed this brief note with her full name. She had written many others and then ripped them to pieces. Some had been quite long letters, reminding him of their life together, and some shorter, full of swearwords and curses. She tore them all up, one after another. In the end, she couldn't stand worrying about it anymore.

Sofia stayed in Hussein's place until almost midnight. She shouldn't have been walking home alone. The village was dark now, apart from fires outside a few houses. The leopard could be around, but she wasn't that afraid of it. Leopards usually avoided people. The only time to be scared was when you came across one unexpectedly in the dark.

The nearer she got to the house, the more nervous she felt. If Armando was still there, she'd hide in the dark until he left. When she could make out the house in the distance, her heart began hammering in her chest. The fire in the front yard was still burning.

She went closer step by step. Lokko didn't come to meet her. Had Armando taken the dog with him?

The yard was empty.

———

Lydia wasn't there.

The door was closed. Sofia stayed in the shadows for a long time, scanning the yard. Then she walked toward the fire.

Now she noticed. No bags.

Armando had been and gone.

CHAPTER

SOFIA TRIED THE DOOR HANDLE, but the door was locked. It was barred from inside. She listened and knocked. Lydia's voice came from inside.

"Who's that?"

"It's me. Sofia."

Lydia let her in, then barred the door again. She seemed frightened. A burning candle had been put on a stool and shadows trembled on the walls. Sofia took the candle with her to her own room. Her three children were sleeping and she sighed with relief.

"Ma, why have you locked the door?"

"Sit down."

Sofia settled on the chilly floor, close to Lydia. Both spoke quietly to avoid waking the children.

"Why lock the door?" Sofia asked again. "What frightened you?"

Lydia started to speak. Sofia realized that her mother was very upset.

"Armando arrived, just as he always does. I showed

him the bags and gave him the letter. He went mad! He shouted at me, and demanded to know where you were. When I said I didn't know, he threatened me. He said he'd beat me up if I didn't tell him. The children became afraid and started crying. Mrs. Mukulela came running and asked him to calm down. Then he threatened her as well. He was going to hit us both until one of us told him where you had gone. In the end he believed me, but it didn't stop him shouting at me. He kept saying he'd get his father and his brothers to come here. They'd throw us out of the house. He was going to stay here with his children. You and me and your little brothers could get lost. When I told him that it was actually you who had paid for the house, he became even angrier. He was a *man*. Neither of us could stop him from throwing us out. *He* was in charge. He carried on like that for hours. Then he grabbed his things and left. He said so many awful things."

"Like what?"

"I don't want to say."

"You must. All this is about me."

"I don't want to."

"Ma, you know I won't leave you alone until you tell me exactly what he said. All of it."

Lydia looked at her and made a face.

"How come you're always so stubborn? There hasn't been anyone in our family as stubborn as you before."

"I'm like that because I have to be. And now I want to know what he said. I guess it was bad things about me."

"He said that you should be grateful that he had allowed himself to make children with a cripple. That you ought to kneel down in front of him, if you had any knees, that is."

Sofia bit her lip to distract herself from the sharp feeling of pain. She didn't want to believe what she heard, but knew it was the truth. Armando hated her now. He wanted to destroy her and go off to live with another woman. And he might try to take her children away from her.

"What else did he say?"

"Isn't that enough?"

"I want to know everything."

Lydia cringed. She wanted to avoid this part of the story, but Sofia had no intention of letting her off. However badly it hurt, she had to know.

"He said that you were mean. That you were no good at bringing up his children. He said he wanted another woman to look after them."

"What else?"

"Nothing more."

"Come on, you said he was hollering for hours on end. He must have thought of something more to say."

"He kept saying the same things over and over again. And, in the end, he just went away. I locked the door, because I was afraid that he'd come back with his brothers."

Sofia tried to think clearly and control her growing bitterness at what Armando had said about her. At the same time, she felt afraid. What if he carried out his threats?

"You were right to lock the door," she said. "From now on, we'll keep it locked every night. Also, Leonardo and Maria mustn't be allowed to run off to play on their own."

Suddenly, Lydia's eyes filled with tears.

"I hope you won't come to regret this. I can't believe the way our family ends up in one hell after another."

Lydia hardly ever used such strong words.

Sofia knew what she meant. There seemed to be no end to the misery they had to endure. The dead children, the poverty, the times they had been almost without food to put in their mouths, the times they were sick and too short of money to pay for the right medicines.

"I won't regret anything," Sofia said.

SOFIA SLEPT BADLY THAT NIGHT. She lay awake, listening for sounds. Wasn't that someone moving about outside? When she fell asleep at last, she thought she saw Armando come toward her. But he was half man, half leopard. His feet were paws and his hands ended in long claws...

At dawn, she woke with a start. The pale gray light behind the curtain told her that the sun was almost up over the horizon. The children slept and from the other room came the noise of Lydia's snoring. Sofia needed to pee. She sat up, strapped on her legs, dressed, took her crutches, and went outside. Lokko came to meet her, wagging his tail. He followed her to the toilet and waited until she had finished.

When she came back to the house, Armando was standing in the yard. Lokko ran up to him, but his master didn't bend down to pat him. Instead Armando gave the dog a kick. Lokko howled and ran off.

Sofia's heart had started to beat very fast the moment she saw Armando. He must have been waiting for her to wake up.

"Armando, don't kick my dog."

"I kick your dog the same way that you kick me."

"I don't kick you!"

"Aren't you kicking me out of here?"

"You've done it yourself. Go to your Eliza. Pet her dog, if she has one."

They stood far apart while they talked. Sofia was shaking. Would he threaten her? Were his father and brothers around, out of sight?

Suddenly Armando came closer to her. Then he burst into tears.

Sofia stared at him. The tears pouring down his

cheeks were real. The man who had bad-mouthed her so dreadfully yesterday, and threatened her mother, was crying his heart out.

"I can't live without you," he said. "I want to be here, with you. I promise I won't see that woman again."

A lump rose in Sofia's throat. But he had said all this before, and made promises he hadn't kept.

"How can I trust you?"

"I swear to you."

"You've done that once already. And it made no difference."

"But this time it is different."

Sofia wanted to believe him. She was very nearly ready to reach out and dry his tears with her hand. Then, in her mind's eye, she saw him once more walking beside the long-legged city woman.

What was it he had said? That I, a cripple, should be grateful because he had given me children?

"I'd like you to leave. Maybe we'll talk about things later. Not now."

LYDIA OPENED THE DOOR cautiously. She saw Armando standing there and then noticed that Sofia waved her back into the house. She obeyed and closed the door again.

Rosa had woken up and was whimpering, but Sofia ignored it. First of all, she had to make sure that Armando understood how serious she was.

———

"Later? When is later?" he asked.

"I don't know. I need more time. But we need to talk about us."

"Do you promise?"

"I promise. But not now. Wait for a month."

"It's too long to wait."

"Then come home two weeks from now."

"Do you promise?"

"I'm always here. We'll talk then."

Armando kept asking her to promise that she really would talk to him. And she kept saying, yes, she would. Finally, when he was about to leave, he reached out to hug her, but she twisted out of the way.

"I love you," he said.

Sofia didn't answer. She turned away and stood listening to his footsteps in the sand. When she looked over her shoulder, he was gone.

She had to sit down. Her body was covered in sweat.

Lydia opened the door again. Once she was sure that Armando was no longer around, she came outside with Rosa in her arms. She handed the baby to Sofia and, while she fed Rosa, Sofia explained what she and Armando had agreed to. They would discuss everything two weeks from now.

Lydia was relieved.

"What you're saying is that he'll be back to live with us?"

———

"No," Sofia said. "Only that we're going to talk. After all, we've brought three children into the world together."

Two weeks passed.

For Sofia, the time dragged. She worked at her sewing machine for as long as she could each day. It was her way to stop herself from thinking about what had happened, mourning lost love, and reliving her anger about what Armando had said about her. She went through all her bits of leftover material and inspected all their old clothes to see what needed to be remade. She sewed clothes for the children and a new blouse for herself.

One day Sofia went to visit Filipinho, the neighbor who had installed electricity in his house. They went outside to sit and talk in the shade of a tree, away from the noise of the tv and his large family. She told him of the plan to save up for two poles and then ask the electricity company to run a cable to her house.

Filipinho smiled at her. He was a bald, big-bellied man, a little worn by a tough life.

"Will you have enough money to do it?" he asked.

"I'm not sure," Sofia said. "But I'd like to try."

She had been quite shocked to learn how much Filipinho had paid for his electricity supply. How on earth would she manage?

"What's your man's name again? Armando, isn't it? Are his wages really good enough?"

Sofia didn't reply. A little later, she got ready to leave.

"Electricity is a very good thing," Filipinho said happily. "Nowadays, we can't remember what it was like to live without light and television."

Sofia went home feeling down. When Armando walked out, her dream of electricity went with him. What was left for her?

She looked around her: this was what was left for her, this village. It was just that she had held on to her hopes for the future, and they were fading now. And then she remembered the blue sand slipping out of her grasp in her dream.

Should she forgive Armando after all? Deep in her heart she knew it was impossible. There was no way back.

AT THE END OF THE TWO WEEKS, Sofia had decided to tell him exactly that.

From early that Sunday morning, she waited for him. She waited until the evening. He never came. She was disappointed, but told herself that she might just as well wait for another week. Had he realized by now that she meant what she said?

When she went to bed that night, she felt a little relieved. She knew she had done the right thing. Her life with Armando was finished. Let him carry on with Eliza.

———

It's a fresh start for the rest of my life, she thought. And not for the first time, either.

SHE EXPECTED TO SEE HIM the following Sunday. On the Friday, a car drove up along the road. Sofia recognized it at once. It was the car Armando had borrowed to drive her to the hospital.

But it wasn't Armando. The man behind the wheel was Samuel, the owner of the car repair shop. He climbed out and said hello. Like everyone in the city, he seemed to be in a hurry and didn't want to sit down when Lydia brought him their only chair with a proper back.

"Sofia Alface," Samuel said. "I'm looking for your husband."

"He isn't here."

Samuel looked troubled.

"If he isn't here, where is he?"

"Isn't he working? He hasn't been here for the last two weeks."

Samuel looked surprised.

"Not for two weeks? Where has he gone?"

"I don't know. Hasn't he been at work?"

Samuel shook his head and Sofia watched him uneasily.

"Armando has been off work for a week. I thought he was sick. That's why I came to see you."

Sofia told him when Armando had come to see them, but didn't mention anything about an argument. That was none of Samuel's business. She assumed that Armando was at home with Eliza. Not that it explained why he wasn't working.

"Some tools have gone missing," Samuel said. "A hammer, a crowbar, a chisel. I don't want to think that Armando had taken them."

This upset Sofia.

"Armando isn't a thief."

"I didn't say he was. I want to know where he is, that's all."

"Perhaps he has gone to see his people, his father or brothers or someone," Lydia suggested.

"No, he hasn't," Samuel replied. "I've looked into that already. His family knows nothing about him either. Has he ever said anything to you about going to South Africa to look for a job?"

"No," Sofia said. "He has never said anything like that.'

Samuel turned to leave.

"I hope nothing bad has happened. I would really like him back, you know. I need him. And I need the tools, if he took them."

Sofia walked with Samuel to the car. He climbed in, but didn't start the engine. There was something on his mind. Then he looked up at Sofia.

"These tools, now," he said. "There's something special about them."

"What's that?"

"They are the kind burglars often use. But I hope I'm wrong."

He started the engine.

"Armando's no thief!" Sofia shouted after the car as it drove off in a cloud of dust.

Afterward, she stood there thinking about what Samuel had said. She felt more and more worried. When she told Armando that she wouldn't live with him, had his grief been genuine? Had he been so upset that he left his job and went off on his own?

Things were going from bad to worse.

Lydia wanted to say something, but Sofia cut her short and she backed away.

Sofia couldn't even be bothered with Lokko. When he came trotting along to be petted, she pushed him away with one of her crutches. Me and Armando alike, she thought. We take our bad mood out on the dog.

THAT EVENING, SOFIA MADE UP HER MIND to do something that would have been unthinkable before Samuel's visit. She would travel to the city and go to see the woman called Eliza. It suddenly seemed very important to find out what Armando was doing. If Samuel didn't know, maybe Eliza did.

———

But, of course, Sofia wanted answers to many other questions. What was she like, the woman Armando had been attracted to? What did she have that Sofia didn't? Except for her nice legs, that is.

THE NEXT DAY, SHE SET OUT EARLY with Rosa on her back.

"Do you really know what you're doing?" Lydia asked.

"Yes, Ma," Sofia said. "This time I know exactly what I'm doing."

Sofia was lucky. Early in her travels, at the place where the overcrowded buses from Swaziland stopped, a car pulled in beside her. She recognized the driver at once. He was Father Ricardo, the Catholic priest, who was famous for his terrible driving. The older he got, the faster and shakier it became. But Sofia risked climbing into his car, because when her baby daughter was with her, she felt nothing could really harm either of them. If there were a God somewhere, He wouldn't be cruel enough to harm Rosa or rob her of her mother.

But it was a tough journey. Father Ricardo had confused her with her sister Rosa. Sofia told him who she was and reminded him that Rosa had been dead for many years, but somehow he still didn't get it. During the whole erratic drive, he kept taking her for her sister.

When they got near the city, Father Ricardo drove off

in the wrong direction and seemed to have forgotten why he was there and where he wanted to go. Sofia asked him to stop when they were quite near Samuel's workshop. She thanked him for the ride and watched as he lurched back into the heavy stream of traffic.

God is really with him, she thought. In his place, I would've crashed the car many times over by now.

WHEN SHE ARRIVED AT THE HOUSE, she felt no trace of nervousness. Once, she had seen Armando and Eliza go inside. Once, she had stood in this street, ready to break a window and throw a burning newspaper through the hole. Now, her own calm surprised her. Surely it should make her both anxious and angry to have to face meeting the woman Armando cared for more than herself?

She checked the house from the other side of the street. It seemed empty. The door and windows were closed. No children were playing outside. She crossed the street, opened the gate, and knocked on the door. Once, twice. Disappointed, she thought that nobody was home.

Then the door suddenly opened. It was Eliza, who eyed Sofia watchfully. This time, Eliza wore long pants, and her hair was styled in a new way, a simple cut.

Suddenly, Sofia became confused. Despite having planned everything so carefully, she didn't know what to say.

"Who are you?" Eliza asked.

———

"I'm the woman who lives with Armando," Sofia replied. "The mother of his children."

Eliza looked startled, but kept staring at Sofia.

"You're lying," she said. "Armando doesn't have any children."

"Is that what he has told you?"

"Armando has no one in the world except me."

Sofia felt dizzy. She had imagined all kinds of things that Eliza might say, but not this. That Armando would have lied about Sofia and their children had been unthinkable. As if they didn't exist! Sofia had to hold onto the wall to stop herself from falling. When Eliza saw this, she took Sofia's arm, led her into the house, and made her sit down.

Eliza went off to get a glass of water and Sofia, left on her own for a moment, had time to recover.

"I'm better now," she said and sipped the water.

Eliza sat down.

"Who are you?"

A cloud of perfume floated around Eliza. Armando used to smell of cinnamon. Was that what attracted them to each other? Scents?

"My name is Sofia," she said.

"What do you want?"

"I want to talk with you about Armando."

"Why?"

"Because it's necessary."

———

"Do you know where he is?"

The question astonished Sofia. That was exactly what she had been about to ask Eliza.

"No," she replied. "I don't know where he is. I've come to ask you the same thing."

They stared at each other, alert as two animals that are unsure if the other is friend or foe.

"Who are you?" Eliza asked again.

"I am Sofia. Armando and I have three children together."

Sofia had brought a small plastic wallet with pictures of her two older children. She handed the wallet to Eliza.

"The boy is called Leonardo," she explained. "The girl's name is Maria. And this little one here is Rosa. She's not one year old yet."

For what seemed a long time, Eliza looked at the photos and at Rosa.

"I don't believe you," she said in the end.

But Sofia could hear the doubt in Eliza's voice and decided that she might as well explain everything, from beginning to end. She told the whole story of the life she and Armando had built together. Then, one day, she had seen him hand in hand with Eliza.

Eliza listened, all the time slowly shaking her head. Sofia didn't need to repeat what she had said. By now Sofia was convinced that Armando had made up a false life for himself, a life without a family of his own.

———

When she had fallen silent, Eliza kept shaking her head.

"I can't take all this in," she said. "He never told me anything about all this. Nothing about you, or the children."

"He left town most Saturdays. He surely explained where he went?"

"He said he visited his parents."

"Where did he say they lived?"

"Along the road to Xai-Xai."

Sofia sighed. He had lied even about this. Xai-Xai and their village were in quite different directions.

Eliza couldn't quite believe that what she had just heard was true. It didn't surprise Sofia, who knew only too well what it is like to confront a lie that only grew bigger as you examined it. The more the two women talked together, the more clearly Armando emerged as a practiced liar. Nothing he had told Eliza was true. He had even said that his mother had died. That was a lie, too.

Armando had been living two separate lives: one with Sofia and another with Eliza.

Eliza said that she was a hairdresser. The house she stayed in belonged to her brother, who would soon return from South Africa. She would have to move out then, because her brother had many children. Armando had promised her that he would buy an apartment for the two of them.

———

"Where would he get the money from?" Sofia asked.

"His sister. She earns a lot of money, he said, because she works for a big company in Europe."

"Armando doesn't have a sister in Europe," said Sofia. "And none of his relatives has any money. Eliza, do you have any idea where he is?"

"No, I don't."

"When did you last see him?"

"A week ago."

"Exactly one week?"

"More like ten days. He was supposed to come here on Saturday, the week before last. He didn't want me to meet him where he worked, you know, fixing cars. But when he didn't turn up, I went there all the same and asked for him. That's when they said that, for all they knew, he had vanished."

Sofia felt anxiety growing inside her again. Where had he gone? And what about Samuel's missing tools? What did it all mean?

"Can't you think of anywhere he might be?" Sofia pleaded.

"I haven't got a clue. I'm not like Armando, I don't tell lies. If his name is Armando, that is. Maybe he lied about that, too?"

"No, he's called Armando all right. How did you two meet?"

"In the street. I was out walking with a couple of

friends and one of them knew Armando, because he had repaired her dad's car. We chatted and got on well. That's all."

Suddenly Sofia felt sorry for her. Her resentment faded away. Eliza had been cheated, just like she had.

"I don't have a phone," Sofia said as she got up from her chair. "And I live far away, in a village off the road toward South Africa and Swaziland. Armando's parents live there, too. There's a man called Hassan in the village who has a phone. Please call this number and leave a message for me if Armando turns up again. Look, I'll leave some money."

She handed a few coins to Eliza, who kept the note with Hassan's number, but refused the money.

"I can afford a phone call. I don't earn a lot, but that's okay at least. What makes you say *when* Armando turns up? What if he doesn't?"

"I can't be sure. But after all, he has three children. People don't simply disappear. He probably hopes that we'll miss him and forget all his lies. Then he'll come back."

Eliza came along to the door. She glanced surreptitiously at Sofia's artificial legs. Sofia noticed and told Eliza about the accident, about Maria's death and all she herself had endured. And it could be that she exaggerated her suffering just a little.

They said good-bye at the gate.

———

"I am very sorry," Eliza said.

"I'm sorry, too," Sofia replied. "But at least you know more about Armando now than you did before."

IT WAS LATE IN THE AFTERNOON. Sofia wanted to get home as soon as possible, but the journey by bus and truck was slow. It was dark when she arrived.

Lydia was sitting by the fire, waiting. When she heard Sofia's footsteps, she jumped up, called Lokko, and went to meet her.

Sofia knew at once that something had happened.

"The police have been here," Lydia said. "They asked if any of us had seen Armando."

"Why?"

"They didn't say. But he must've done something."

"Didn't they hint at anything?"

"No. They came in a car and had driven all the way from the city just to get hold of him. When I said he wasn't here, they went away again."

Sofia felt the worry-snake starting to crawl in her belly after having been quiet for the last few hours.

What had Armando done? What had happened?

9

AFTER A SLEEPLESS NIGHT, Sofia traveled to the city again.

Armando had caused her so much pain, but now he needed help. Help of a kind only she could offer him. During the night, all her fears and all the anger she had felt because he had left her and the children had changed into a different mixture of feelings: she was still upset, but also deeply worried about what he might do next. Had he stolen the tools after all? Was he turning into a thief? Was there a risk that Leonardo, Maria, and Rosa would see their father in prison?

I don't want my children to grow up knowing that their dad is a thief, she kept telling herself, as she sat crammed into the bus that slowly shook and bumped its way to the city. I can help him, she thought, and still make him understand that I won't forgive him for the way he has hurt me.

The first thing she did after getting off the bus in the city was to go looking for the hairdressing salon where

Eliza worked. When they had talked, Eliza had mentioned the name of the street. Sofia kept asking directions from people she met. Her hips were sore after the bus ride and walking on city sidewalks made the ache worse. But she had no intention of giving up. She would find Eliza and then Armando.

A few hours later, after looking in on several salons just in case, she finally arrived at the right place. She saw Eliza right away, massaging the scalp of a woman who had fallen asleep, and caught her eye. Eliza asked somebody else to look after the sleepy customer and went over to Sofia.

They went outside to talk. Sofia told her that the police had arrived in the village yesterday, looking for Armando, and that they had questioned her mother. She added that Samuel suspected Armando of stealing some tools, which could be a burglar's kit.

Eliza shook her head.

"He must've made a mistake," she said. "It's not like Armando."

"I believed he would never abandon me, but I know better now. He has lied to me and lied to you, too. Neither of us can do anything about it. But I don't want my children to grow up with a thief for a father."

"Let's go to Samuel's place and talk to him."

Eliza went into the salon and quickly came back with her bag slung over her shoulder.

"That old woman is still asleep," she said with a grin. "In our salon we all help each other out when someone needs it."

"Let's go!" said Sofia. "I'm thirsty. And hungry, too."

A TEA SELLER HAD STARTED TO BOIL WATER over the fire he had built next to a fallen tree on the sidewalk. They bought mugs of tea, ate some bananas, and talked, mostly trying to figure out where Armando could be. Neither of them could think of a likely place.

At the workshop, Samuel was sitting in the shade, flicking his handkerchief at the flies while he shouted instructions to a young man who was fiddling with something under the hood of a truck.

When he saw them, he rose at once and offered them a place to sit in the yard behind his shop, where someone had set up a few old car seats under a torn garden umbrella. He seemed worried and listened gravely when Sofia told him about the police coming to look for Armando.

"What can the boy have been up to?" he asked when she had finished. "It's as if he has changed into someone different from the person he used to be."

Sofia decided to be honest with him.

"Armando and I had a fight. I had discovered that he was going out with another woman."

She didn't say that the woman was Eliza, but Samuel probably understood that anyway.

"Then what happened?" he asked.

"I threw him out. I left two bags with his clothes."

"And?"

"I told him we'd talk once a few weeks had passed."

Samuel nodded.

"Now I understand a bit better. You see, I noticed something was up one Monday morning a while ago. He was here and working as usual, but in an odd mood. Somehow not with you."

Samuel couldn't suggest a place where Armando might be. He questioned all the mechanics, one by one, but no one seemed to know Armando well, or have any idea where he might be.

"Does he have any relatives in the city?" Samuel asked in the end.

"I can't say for certain," Sofia said. "It's as if I knew nothing about him."

"Suddenly, he has vanished," said Samuel. "His parents know as little as the rest of us."

"Could he be off to South Africa?" Eliza asked.

Samuel nodded.

"That's possible. We can't do anything except wait and hope he isn't up to something he shouldn't be."

"I wonder why the police wanted to get hold of him," Sofia said. "They must have a reason."

"There are thousands of police officers in this city and just a couple of them turned up in your village. We haven't got any chance of finding them."

Sofia knew he was right and tapped impatiently on the base of the umbrella with one of her crutches. This was unbearable. Just hanging around, waiting. Was there really nothing she could do?

Samuel seemed to read her thoughts.

"Wait is all we *can* do," he said. "Even if it's the last thing we want."

SOFIA LEFT THAT AFTERNOON. Eliza walked with her to the bus terminal. Life can take strange turns, Sofia thought. A few weeks ago, she had hated Eliza and been prepared to burn her house down. Now, they were good friends.

ONCE AGAIN, SOFIA FOUGHT HER WAY into one of the packed buses. Through the dirty window she spotted a few shiny, black cars going past, with one or two passengers inside. These people had space to themselves.

Being poor means that you're always in a crowd, she thought. I must write that down in my diary.

THAT EVENING, SOFIA TALKED WITH LYDIA. She no longer felt the need to keep her mother out of her life with Armando. She depended very much on Lydia's support, especially so she wouldn't lose her patience completely.

They sat by the fire after the children had gone to bed. They could hear Mrs. Mukulela humming a song outside her house.

"We mustn't believe the worst of Armando," Lydia said. "He's usually such a good and sensible young man. Don't forget that's why you wanted to live with him in the first place."

"I don't forget anything. It's just that I can't help worrying."

Lydia nodded silently and Sofia understood. If there was one person in the world who knew about worrying, it was Lydia.

IT TOOK SOFIA A VERY LONG TIME TO FALL ASLEEP. She was tired, but twisted about in bed for several hours before she finally got to sleep. In her dreams, she was running in a great darkness. She was looking for Armando, but couldn't find him.

Something made a scratching noise on the wall of the house. Lokko? He often rubbed himself against the rough surface to get rid of itchy insects. The sound continued. Slowly, Sofia dragged herself awake, opened her eyes, and listened into the night. Scratch, scratch, scratch. And now something was tapping lightly on the windowpane. It scared her and her heart beat faster.

———

Silence. Then she heard the faint scraping again.

She hauled herself to the bottom of the bed and pulled the curtain back. The moon was bright.

Armando stood outside. The blue light almost made him look the same as when she had seen him for the first time. He made a sign for her to come out. She couldn't see his face clearly, but knew that he was upset. She let go of the curtain, strapped on her legs, and dressed quickly. Just before opening the door, she stood still for a moment in the silent house.

Why had he come? What did he want? And why come in the middle of the night?

She sensed danger. But what could be dangerous? After all, it seemed that nothing serious had happened to him. He was here, just outside the door.

She stepped into the moonlight. Armando was standing near the dead fire with Lokko at his feet. The night was warm. Insects were dancing in the air around Sofia's face.

She walked toward him. His face was hidden in the shadows.

"Armando, what do you want?"

"I want to come home."

"Where have you been? What have you done? The police have been here and asked about you."

"I haven't done anything."

"Samuel has been asking about you, too. He says

you're not coming in to work. And besides, some of his tools have gone missing. The kind of tools burglars use, he thinks."

She still couldn't make out his face, but heard the tension in his voice.

"I can't work. Not now, the way things are between us."

"You have three children to support, Armando. And I don't want our children's father to be a thief."

"I haven't stolen any tools. I'm not a burglar."

"Why come here in the middle of the night?"

He avoided the question. Instead, he took hold of her arm and pointed. A car was parked on the side of the road. It gleamed in the moonlight and looked just like the cars she had seen through the bus window, one of the ones with just a few people inside.

She felt scared again.

"Have you stolen that car?"

"I borrowed it."

"Samuel doesn't repair cars like that!"

"I've got a new job. The pay is very good and I'm allowed to borrow this car whenever I like."

His voice sounded convincing. But could she risk believing him? She wasn't sure, only felt more and more confused.

"I'd like to show you where I work," he said.

"Now? In the middle of the night?"

———

"You refuse to see me in the daytime. And the trip won't take more than an hour."

"Where are we going?"

"It's a surprise."

"Only an hour?"

"I swear. No more."

This is crazy, Sofia thought. All the same, she followed him down to the road and climbed into the car. Could she trust him now? More than anything else, she wanted to know what had happened since he disappeared. There must be a reason why the police were looking for him.

"One hour," she said. "No more."

"I promise."

Armando started the engine. Instantly, cool air blew against her face. Lights blinked on a car radio. It was set to a music station. The car seat was soft. It felt like sitting on a chair made for a queen.

Queen Sofia, she thought. But Armando is no king.

He left the village and swung onto the main road. Sofia waited for him to say something, but he stayed silent. Suddenly he pressed the accelerator. The car gained speed. The beams of the headlights were cutting through the darkness.

"Don't drive so fast," Sofia said. "Not this fast."

Armando seemed not to hear. Now he drove faster still.

———

He'll kill both of us, Sofia thought. Dear God, that's why he came for me. He's going to drive us both to our deaths in a stolen car!

She panicked.

"I'll do anything you like," she said. "But please don't drive so fast."

He lowered the speed at once. As if nothing had really happened.

"Where are we going?"

"To my cousin's house."

"I didn't know you had a cousin."

"Hasn't everyone?"

"Who's he? What's he called?"

"Sergio."

"Why haven't you ever told me about him? Where does Sergio live?"

"Along this road."

"Armando, I don't want you to drive so fast."

"I'm not driving very fast."

Armando slowed down again. Suddenly, he turned off the main road and took the car down a smaller road. To Sofia, it looked more like a tractor track between fields. Ahead, in the headlights, lay empty land and they were driving straight into it.

"Does your cousin really live out here?"

Armando didn't reply. Sofia began to get frightened again and regretted coming with him. Why couldn't she ever learn to make the right decisions? Why did she say yes, when she ought to say no?

The drive continued for perhaps twenty minutes. Armando didn't say a word. Sofia could see no houses, nor any other signs of people.

Suddenly, Armando put his foot down hard on the brake and stopped the engine. He left the headlights on and turned on a light in the ceiling. Sofia saw that he looked pale and exhausted, that his hair was messy and his eyes bloodshot. She sensed something wild and haunted about him. He also smelled, maybe of the liquor that people brewed from corn or rice.

"You don't have a cousin called Sergio," Sofia said. "What do you want from me?"

"I want to come home."

"We've talked about that already. Not now, not yet."

Armando shook his head.

"I can't wait. I want to come back home now."

"This car, who does it belong to?"

"I've told you that already."

"I don't believe you."

Armando suddenly switched the car light off and then the headlights. The moon had gone behind a cloud and darkness surrounded them. Sofia felt afraid again. When Armando leaned close to her, the smell of alcohol was stronger. His voice changed, grew tense, more dangerous.

———

"All I want is to come home. Nothing else."

"Not now."

Armando turned the car light on again. His face was very close to hers.

"If you don't let me come home now, I'll leave you in this place. Out here, no one will find you. You'll die."

"Why do you say that?"

"I say it because I'm your man. Nobody does to me what you've done."

Sofia was taken aback, then felt angry as well as frightened.

"What have *I* done? *You* are the one who has done something wrong, not me."

"I want us to forget what has happened."

"I can't. Not yet."

Armando switched the car light off again. Sofia wondered if he was like this just because he was drunk, or if something was going wrong inside his head. He was so strange. She made up her mind to stop talking to him. The only thing she should do now was to make him drive her home.

She waited. The darkness outside seemed to seep into the car through invisible pores. She listened to Armando's strained breathing. He's not himself, she thought.

"Do you want to know about the car?" he asked suddenly.

Sofia didn't reply. Once again, his voice changed. It

———

sounded colder now, harder, more determined.

"Do you want to know about the car?" he said again. "Here goes. I stole it. I took a screwdriver, bent it in half, and fixed it to a small wrench. It looked like a gun in the dark. I took this car from a man, a white man, when he stepped out of a restaurant. He was drunk by then. The guy must've been rich. I wanted the gun to be real then, so I could shoot him. Maybe I would've. Anyway, I drove off in his car. It's a good one. I'll spray it a new color and change the license plates. I can sell it for more money than I'd get in ten years working for Samuel. Do you understand what I'm saying? Ten years! I want us to have a good life together now. You and I fight because we're poor, that all."

"We fight because you lie and steal," Sofia said. "I want you to drive me home. Now!"

The clouds drew apart and suddenly the moonlight was back. Sofia could see Armando's face, but he was no longer Moon Boy. He was someone else, someone she didn't know.

"I'll leave you here," he said. "Unless you promise me that everything will be good between us from now on."

Sofia couldn't believe him. Anger rose inside her again, even though she knew that she should stay calm.

"Drive me home. I'm fed up with this."

Things happened very quickly. Armando leapt out of

the car and ran to the other side. He pulled Sofia out, let her fall on the ground, and threw the crutches at her.

"I hope the lions come for you!" he screamed. "Or the leopards! Or the snakes or the jackals!"

The car drove off with a roar. She watched as the beams of the headlights grew more distant and then disappeared altogether.

The moon hid behind thickening clouds. The landscape was utterly silent. It had all been so quick that only now did she realize what had happened.

She was alone, deep in the bush. There were no people here, only wild animals prowling or crawling about, hunting for food.

Panic paralyzed her. Armando could not have done this. He wanted to scare her, that was all. He'd come back for her soon.

But however hard she scanned the darkness, she couldn't see any lights, or pick up the sound of a car engine from anywhere.

He wouldn't come back.

She was on her own. It was clear to her that Armando had really changed. He was sick in the head. Nothing else could explain the way he had left her in the middle of the night, so far from other people and in this place where lions and leopards, hyenas and wild dogs stalked.

———

Sofia had never before in her life felt so frightened and so lonely. She prayed silently to the gods and to Ma Lydia, but she was and remained alone. And dawn was many hours away.

There was a tree close by and Sofia started to heave herself up into it. By the time she had reached a branch that was high enough to offer some safety, her arms and face were full of deep scratches. In her heart she knew this wouldn't help her if wild animals came for her. And snakes sometimes hid in the tops of trees. Still, she had to do what she could to get away from the dangers surrounding her.

The minutes dragged past. At times she was convinced that she heard the heavy breathing of a lion or a leopard close by. Predators were watching her, but she couldn't see them.

At some point during that long night, she remembered how once, ten years ago, she had been left alone in a wheelchair outside the hospital. She had just lost her legs and was waiting to be fitted with artificial legs. People had simply forgotten about her. She had been very frightened, but not like this time.

Here, every moment could be her last. Every moment could be the one when a wild animal would be ready to spring at her. She held on tightly to the crutches so that she would have something to defend herself with when it happened.

——

It was the longest night of her life. When morning finally dawned as a streak of gray light on the horizon, she burst into tears. Daylight would make the wild animals of the night withdraw. Now she could go in search of people who could help her.

She climbed down from the tree and started walking, following the car tracks. She was on a large prairie, covered in shrubby undergrowth and scattered with solitary trees. After walking for about an hour, she reached a track and a little later, she heard a tractor. That moment she felt sure that she would be all right after all.

The tractor driver was a young man, who stopped to pick her up. When he asked why she was walking here, alone and on crutches, she told him that she had been kidnapped.

He asked nothing more, but Sofia knew that he was afraid, fearful that he had offered a ride to a supernatural being who might be dangerous.

When she got home, Lydia was talking with Mrs. Mukulela outside the house. They had been frightened for her and were very relieved to see her walking toward them along the road.

"Don't ask me anything," Sofia said. "I'm so tired. I must sleep. But I'm well. Nothing bad has happened."

Before resting, she had to feed her baby.

As soon as she was in bed, she realized that sleep was

impossible. It was as if she was still clutching the branches of the tree, waiting for wild animals to attack her.

Leonardo stood in the doorway and looked at her. Sofia reached out her hand to him and he came closer. She could see how upset he was.

"Everything will be all right now," she said.

He looked doubtful.

"Everything will be all right," she said again. "Run off and play!"

He went away. Sofia closed her eyes. Sleep still wouldn't come.

Suddenly, she sat straight up. A sudden thought, little more than an impulse, had come from nowhere, but she knew immediately that it was important.

A great danger was looming. Whatever Armando had done, she had to find him soon, or it would be too late.

Too late for what? She didn't know, but she was convinced that she had to find him.

Danger threatened him.

———

CHAPTER

10

ELIZA WAS AT HOME WHEN SOFIA ARRIVED with Rosa on her back.

It was still early in the morning. Sofia had left the village before dawn and caught one of the first buses to the city.

Eliza was packing her two suitcases, because she had to move out of the house that afternoon to make room for her brother and his family.

"Tomorrow morning I would've been gone," she said, once Sofia had sat down to rest.

"Look, we both forgot," Sofia told her. "I mean, you to give me your address and me to remind you of it."

Eliza scribbled a note on a torn-off piece of paper. *Bairo de Jardim*. Sofia knew roughly where it was. It was one of the poorest areas of the city, where most of the houses were without water and electricity.

Eliza lives as I do, Sofia thought. Did Armando seek his women among the poor? Or had he believed that Eliza was well off?

Sofia explained to Eliza about her feeling that Armando was in great danger. Eliza looked skeptical. Sofia began to wonder if she hadn't exaggerated the danger to Armando after all. But she shook off her doubts. She *knew*. The feeling inside her was so strong it had to be true.

"I must find him," she said again.

"I have to be at work today," Eliza told her. "I can't afford to lose my job. There's an invisible lineup of ten more girls just waiting for me to do something stupid and get fired. They'd fight over my job. I can't help you look for him."

Sofia didn't reply. If Eliza was busy, she'd have to find Armando herself.

She looked at the two cases. Eliza was tying the lids down with string.

"He didn't leave anything for you to keep, did he?"

"For me? No, nothing."

"No papers?"

Eliza shook her head. Sofia believed her and understood why. Armando was like a careful animal, leaving no traces.

She rose and stood, supporting herself on the crutches.

"What are you going to do now?" Eliza asked.

"I'll keep looking. I'll let you know when I find him."

——

First, Sofia went to the car workshop. Samuel wasn't in yet. Some mornings he set out early to go hunting for spare car parts in scrap merchants' yards. Sofia left again after learning that Armando had never shown up and that the missing tools hadn't been found.

The day was going to be hot and humid. Perhaps there'd be a thunderstorm before dark. She was pressed for time.

When she arrived at the house where he rented a room, the landlady, a widow called Rosita, refused to let her in.

"You could be anybody. How am I to know that you're really Armando's wife?"

"I *am* his wife," Sofia said and thumped the floor with one of her crutches. "Look, here is his daughter, Rosa."

Señora Rosita was a small, slight woman. Sitting in a worn wicker chair outside her tumbledown house, she was like a shabby, little old dog guarding a well-chewed bone.

Sofia didn't back down. In the end, Señora Rosita believed her and opened the door to the room where Armando had stayed.

"You're not to take anything away," she said before closing the door.

Sofia was alone in the small room. The walls were bare. The only light came from a single bulb in the ceiling. A dirty towel had been stuffed into a broken windowpane. She stood still for a while, taking it all in. Armando's clothes were there. If he had set out for South Africa or somewhere, he wouldn't have left his things. He's here in this city, she thought. He hasn't gone to live in another country.

She found a small notebook on the floor, hidden under the mattress he slept on. She pulled it out and took it to the window to see it better. Page after page was filled with Armando's spiky handwriting. He seemed to have noted down types of cars and rated each one. Here and there were sets of figures, which Sofia assumed were phone numbers. On the last page he had made a note of an address. The person it belonged to must have been some kind of relative: Uncle Simon, it said. She tucked the notebook away under her blouse and left.

Outside in the sunshine, Señora Rosita eyed her suspiciously.

"I didn't take anything," Sofia told her. "If Armando comes back, tell him that I've been here."

"Why shouldn't he come back?" Señora Rosita sounded quite angry. "He has paid the rent for the next month."

Sofia felt better when she heard that. Armando wouldn't have paid the rent if he didn't have to. At least he wasn't planning to go off somewhere else anytime soon.

———

WHEN SHE STARTED THE SEARCH for the uncle who might know where Armando was, Sofia felt better. The anxiety that had driven her was loosening its grip. Was it the possibility of his going far away that she had really feared? That he might never return? Had she been afraid that she and the children would never see him again?

She bought a bottle of water and went to sit in the shade of a tree. She was thirsty and Rosa was hungry. Suddenly, her sense of urgency drained away. No need to push herself so hard, to strain her aching hips. Sitting quietly in the shade, she wondered if Armando hadn't been truly desperate. Maybe all he really wanted was to come home. But my fears and jealousy are real, too, she thought. I have children and can't escape to go looking for another man.

She rested for a little longer and then set out to walk to the suburb where Armando's uncle might live. It was close to the city limits, on the way to the airport, where she and Armando had once watched the planes land and take off. He had never mentioned a relative who lived nearby. There's too much that I don't know about him, she thought.

Her thoughts kept returning to the way Armando had exposed her to terrible danger. How could he? He must answer her before she could even begin to think about letting him come back home.

By midday, Sofia was very tired and her hips felt

worse than ever. She had hoped to get a ride with the trucks taking passengers to the airport, but they were packed with people and didn't stop for her.

IT WAS LATE IN THE AFTERNOON, the hottest time of the day, when she reached the suburb: a mass of shacks along narrow, unpaved alleys with stinking sewage drains. It upset her to see how many city people were as poor as the very poorest in her village.

Sofia asked the few people she met, but no one seemed to know about Armando's uncle. She had a growing sense that something out of the ordinary was going on. Where was everyone? She stopped making her way along the narrow alleyways, listened, and heard the murmur of a distant crowd. Now and then people walked quickly by, pushing to get between Sofia and the walls of the houses. Apart from herself, everyone hurried.

She turned to ask an old man whose legs were paralyzed and who walked slowly with crutches, as she did.

"What's going on?"

"Bad things. But what must be, must be."

Sofia had no idea what he meant and walked on. The noise grew louder and she had a frightening premonition of something horrible about to happen. Suddenly, the labyrinth of houses opened into a square, surrounded by tall piles of garbage. It was filled with a large crowd of people who seemed angry about something. The crowd

160

was growing all the time. She stopped and pressed herself against the wall of a house. Whatever this was about, she didn't want to be involved.

Now the people were shifting, forming an uneven semicircle. Everyone was shouting, roaring, screaming. It was impossible to figure out what it was all about. Then a movement went through the crowd and a path opened up. Through it, a handful of men came running, carrying car tires on their heads.

The roaring noise changed and became more like a growl. Another group of men arrived, dragging between them an almost naked young man. A torn shirt covered his face. His body was bloody.

Next, everything happened very quickly.

The young man's voice rose to piercing shrieks. He kept trying to resist, but nothing could help him now. People were cursing him, calling him a thief and the lowest of the low—someone who stole even from those as poor as himself. If he had to do it, why not steal from rich men? Because he had done what he had done, he deserved no mercy.

Horrified, Sofia saw them put one of the car tires around his neck, pour gas all over him, and set him on fire. He burned like a torch, screaming.

Just as the flames rose around his body, he managed to free his hands and rip the shirt from his face.

Sofia saw what she didn't want to see.

———

It felt as if the fierce sun and the flames burned the image into her eyes. The man on fire was Armando. It was Armando's flailing body, struggling to escape the flames that were tormenting and killing him. Sofia screamed, but no one noticed. She heard people shouting that when a thief among them was caught, this was his punishment. When a poor man steals from the poor, he deserves to die.

Armando collapsed on the ground. After a while he stopped screaming and Sofia stumbled toward him. Rosa, tied on her back, had started to cry, as if she understood something of the horror.

Sofia fell in the sand. She didn't know if Armando was alive or dead. His face was destroyed. He had no eyes, his skin was scorched. The stench of gas and of burning fat and flesh hung over everything.

Someone pulled her away. She screamed and struggled, but the hands that held her were strong and didn't let go. She didn't manage to free herself until some women came over. They asked why she was so upset.

"He's my man! You have killed my husband!"

"He isn't your husband," one of the women said. "He's a thief. We caught him stealing."

Sofia grabbed hold of the shawl on the woman's head and pulled her face closer to her own.

"He's my husband," she said again. "He's my husband, this man you've killed."

———

Now the woman believed her and turned to shout something to the men who were watching the fire and beating the body with long sticks. Someone started to shovel sand over the smouldering corpse. When they had finished, Armando's body lay under what looked like a grave mound. Smoke was seeping through the sand.

Sofia was lying on her side. The sun was hot on her cheek. She didn't notice. What had happened must be a dream. It couldn't be true. Armando was still out there, somewhere. She hadn't found him yet, that was all. The thief they had burned to death must be someone else, anyone, but not Armando...

When she came to, she was inside a shack. Rosa lay next to her, awake but not crying now. A group of men and women stood at the bedside, watching them. As soon as Sofia opened her eyes, she knew what had happened. The dead man had not burned in a dream. He had died in front of her.

She looked up at the people around her. Their eyes were no longer full of rage. It had been replaced by remorse.

In that instant, the last shreds of her disbelief vanished, too. Armando was dead. He was a thief who had been caught and punished. Her fears had proved true. He had become someone else, a thief who no longer cared for her, or their children, or even himself.

She lay still on the hard boards of the bed, trying to drive away the terrible images of Armando's death.

It is as if fire follows me always, all my life, she thought. I learned to see the future in the flames. Fire warms and causes pain; it is unpredictable and mysterious. And sometimes it is full of fury.

An old man sat down beside her.

"They say that it was your husband who died?"

He spoke in a low voice and she saw the sadness in his eyes.

"You killed Armando," she said. "You poured gas over my children's father and set fire to him. What had he done?"

"He had stolen a bicycle."

"You kill for that?"

"I tried to stop them. But people as poor as us become mad with rage when someone takes what little we own."

"You are all crazy. You should be killed, every one of you. If I could, I'd pour gas over all of you and throw a burning match into the crowd."

"I tried to stop what happened."

"If you catch a thief, you go to the police."

"No one could've stopped them."

Sofia knew that he was telling the truth. No thief had ever been killed in her village. But in one of Lydia's stories of past times, a man had his hands cut off for stealing an ox. There were always those who craved revenge, who didn't want to wait for the police, and couldn't get it into their heads that thieves should be put in prison. Among the very poor, fury and revenge are sometimes all that matters. To them, a bicycle can be worth a human life.

"I am sad for you," the old man said. "And ashamed. But there was nothing I could do."

He fell silent. Sofia lay still, staring at the ceiling. More than anything else, she wanted to sleep—sleep for many years, perhaps forever. But terrible images of Armando burning and screaming came back as soon as she closed her eyes.

SOFIA NEVER KNEW HOW THE REST of that day passed. She had lost all sense of time, just lay there on the boards, sipped the water they gave her, heard the sound of people talking quietly outside the shack. The old man stayed by her. Very slowly, the dreadful sight of Armando on fire receded.

Unanswerable questions came and went in her mind. What if I had arrived here a little earlier? What if I had realized that the man was Armando before they poured gas over him?

Then, men in uniform entered. They were police officers and they informed her of Armando's other thefts. He had stolen cars and used weapons to threaten people. This was why they had come looking for him in the village.

165

But if he stole cars, why bother with a bicycle? No one had an answer. The police were furious with the people who had carried out the execution. Several of them would go to prison.

But nothing would bring Armando back to her.

One of the police officers offered to drive her home. Dusk had already fallen when she went outside. The crowd was gone. Smoke no longer seeped from the sandy mound over the scorched remains of Armando's body.

"We'll have him picked up," a police officer said. "The people who've done this should at least be made to pay for his coffin."

Just as Sofia was about to climb into the police car, she turned to the old man who had sat with her and asked about Armando's uncle.

"Simon? He left for South Africa many years ago. We haven't heard from him since."

On the journey home, Sofia sat in the back of the police car and thought about Armando. Had he been disappointed when he realized that Simon had gone to South Africa? Had he stolen a bicycle just to get away as quickly as possible? Perhaps he had planned to go to South Africa after all?

Death posed questions, but never gave answers.

When she got back to her village, she asked to be let

out far away from her house. She didn't want Lydia to find out that the police had brought her home.

Sofia stood still for a while, trying to muster strength. She was certain of one thing: her children would never know their father's fate. They had to be told that he had died, but not that he had been burned as a thief. She didn't intend to tell Lydia the truth either.

I cannot bear any more death, she thought. I can't bear all this dying. It's as if there's less and less room for life.

Standing on the road, she wept. And then she suddenly became aware of Lokko being with her, close to her feet.

"Let's go home now," she said.

THAT EVENING, SITTING ON THE STRAW MAT, she told Lydia that Armando was dead. He had been in an accident. Lydia asked no questions, said little, and wept for a while. Then she wandered off into the darkness. Sofia heard her walking on the road.

No fire was burning that night. Sofia wondered if she would ever again love watching the flames.

Lydia was back. Sofia couldn't see her face. It was as if the darkness was speaking.

"You shouldn't have been so hard on him," she said. "You should have forgiven him."

Sofia became upset, but fearful at the same time.

"What are you saying? That it's my fault that he died?"

"I mean just what I say."

Lydia went into the house. Sofia stayed, sitting in the dark with Lokko. Was Lydia right? If she was, for the rest of her life Sofia would have to bear the guilt of having caused Armando's death.

Life is too hard, she thought. I'm still too young to understand it.

She cried and cried. Lokko crept closer to her.

THE FOLLOWING DAY, Sofia told Leonardo and Maria that their father had died. They probably didn't take in what it meant—that Armando would never again come walking down that road.

Four days later they buried Armando by the river. Armando's parents were there. Sofia had told them that Armando had died in a car accident. Samuel came, and Eliza, but they weren't told the truth either.

SLOWLY, TIME BEGAN TO MOVE ON AGAIN. Sofia visited the grave almost every day. Was she really responsible for the despair that drove Armando to become a thief? She found no answer and her questions kept haunting her. She hoped to hear Armando speak to her from the grave on the riverbank, but no whispers reached her. Maria and Rosa were also silent.

———

She told herself that their silence wouldn't last for all eternity. One day the dead would start talking to her again.

ONE DAY, SAMUEL CAME TO VISIT THEM. Before leaving, he took Sofia aside and gave her a plastic bag.

"We took a collection," he said. "Armando was a good car mechanic. I miss him."

That evening, Sofia counted the money in the bag. It was more than she had ever owned before in her life and almost enough to install electricity in their house.

She made up her mind instantly. That was what she would do.

EPILOGUE

———————

A YEAR PASSED.

It was a long year, the longest Sofia had ever lived through. Every day, she felt as if she must drag a heavy, black stone with her until evening. When darkness fell, there was a brief rest, before she had to start hauling the hours of the night along until the sun rolled up over the horizon again.

In the evenings, when the children slept and Lydia had gone to bed, she almost always sat alone for a while by the fire. Lokko would lie on the other side of the fire, sometimes watching her, sometimes asleep.

She tried to understand how it could have been different. She met Eliza, too. She needed to talk with her, to explain what had really happened, and to try to understand it herself.

Perhaps there was no way to make sense of life. Armando had died. The children had lost their father. Sofia, too, had lost her father, Hapakatanda. He had been killed by bandits.

OLD MRS. MUAZENA, dead for many years now, had once told Sofia and Maria about the secrets of the fire. They often found it hard to understand what she was telling them. Mrs. Muazena was a wise lady, but a little strange. Sometimes she was very clear and sometimes incomprehensible.

"Every fire holds a secret inside it," she had said. "If you sit at the right distance away from the flames you can see so deeply into their dance that you find out what will happen in your life."

Mrs. Muazena pointed with her wrinkled hand out toward the fields where Lydia worked every day.

"In the fields, the plants are lined up in rows," she said. "Every day is a plant, too. A plant for you to look after and help along as best you can. Pull out all poisonous weeds. Later on, you will harvest it. Every day in your life is a plant, a moment you have not yet lived."

YOU NEVER KNOW HOW LONG YOU WILL LIVE, Sofia thought. What of her children, asleep inside? How long would they live? Every evening by the fire, Sofia worried about them. Dangers lay in wait everywhere.

Sometimes she would bring a few of her old diaries with her to read in the firelight. Looking through them, she realized how easy it is to forget the past and also how long she had been pondering the questions that preoccupied her now.

———

"Why am I alive?" Sofia asked Lokko.

He opened his eyes and looked at her. And went back to sleep.

A small beetle crawled over her hand.

"Why am I alive?" Sofia asked.

The beetle kept crawling, and fell off her hand into the sand.

She talked to the stars, to Rosa and Maria, to Mrs. Muazena. Silence. If there were to be any answers, they must come from Sofia herself.

It could be that what is happening to me now is what will teach me to be an adult, she thought. Teach me that there are questions without any answers and that those you come up with, you will have found yourself.

In that year, Leonardo and Maria grew taller, Rosa started walking, and Lydia became more tired and prone to aches in her back and legs. Sofia sewed for people more than ever and saved all she could. She wanted to buy a new electric sewing machine for when they got electricity.

Now and then, Hortensia and Stefano would visit. They married that year. Eliza came, too. Sometimes she would stay for a few extra days to run a hairdressing salon. She would cut and braid the hair of everyone in the village and she charged very little.

Armando's parents were the only people who never

visited. Sofia kept hoping that, for the sake of their grandchildren, they would change their minds one day.

Her hardest task was to explain to Leonardo that his father would never come back. She still hadn't told him what really happened. Leonardo had been very quiet during the first months after Armando's funeral. Sofia kept a watchful eye on him. Sometimes he would ask questions about Armando and she answered as well as she could.

It hurt her to have to lie to her own child. Maybe she would tell him the truth one day, but she wasn't sure. She wasn't sure of anything. Life was uncertain, from the first day to the last. She told herself that she was learning.

But in the middle of her questioning and her grief, she could sometimes feel unexpected joy. Her children were healthy, and something of Armando still lived in them. There were mornings when she woke up with a song inside her. Then she could allow herself to be a little childish again, pat her legs and tell them to work well for her today, there was such a lot to do. She would soon have saved enough money to ask the electricity company to install electric cables.

ON THE ANNIVERSARY OF ARMANDO'S DEATH, Sofia sat by the fire with Lokko for a long time. It had rained during the day and she had to put a double layer of straw matting on the ground. In the night sky the clouds started breaking up, allowing glimpses of a half moon.

It was just the fire, and the dog, and her. The rest of the world seemed empty. The dog slept, the flames danced. She narrowed her eyes and looked into the fire.

There are secrets in there, riddles and fury. Fire warms, but it can burn.

SUDDENLY, SOMETHING INSIDE HER seemed to lighten. A happiness that came from nowhere.

"We're alive," she said to Lokko.

The dog opened his eyes.

"I know," Lokko replied. "We're alive."

Then his eyes closed and his head was back resting on his paw.

My dog is very special, Sofia thought. Sometimes I almost believe he can speak.

She stayed by the fire until it had almost died down. Then she kicked sand over the embers and went inside.

The children slept, Lydia slept, her brothers slept. She stopped, closed her eyes, and listened to all these people breathing.

My family, she thought. Without them I'm nobody.

Then that old feeling came back. She felt surrounded by invisible people. There they were: Maria, Rosa, Doctor Raul, Hapakatanda. Her family was made up not only of the living but also of the dead.

———

Armando too was there, somewhere in the shadows. He belonged with the unseen ones. He would not be forgotten. Soon he would stay...

Sofia stood there for a long time among the dead. She could almost feel them touching her, lightly stroking her face with their fingertips.

In the end, she said good-bye to them all.

THAT NIGHT SHE DREAMED ABOUT A MAN who came along carrying a sewing machine. A man, or was it a woman? Maybe Mrs. Muazena? Or Mrs. Mukulela? It could have been Rosa, or Maria. In her dream she couldn't see very clearly. But the sewing machine, now, there was no doubt about that.

The house slept. The future awaited...

ABOUT THE AUTHOR
AND TRANSLATOR

HENNING MANKELL is one of Sweden's best-selling authors. His books have been translated into thirty-five languages and have sold more than twenty million copies worldwide. He has published a number of plays and novels for adults, including an internationally acclaimed series of detective novels featuring Inspector Kurt Wallander. His books for children and young adults have won him several awards, including the prestigious Astrid Lindgren Prize, and his previous book about Sofia, *Secrets in the Fire*, won the 2002 International Sankei Children's Publishing Culture Award. Henning was born in Stockholm in 1948 and currently divides his time between Sweden and Mozambique.

ANNA PATERSON is an award-winning literary translator of Scandinavian languages and German into English. In 2000, she won the Bernard Shaw Prize for her translation of *Forest of Hours* by Kerstin Ekman, and her translation of *The Exception* by Christian Jungersen was longlisted for the IMPAC award in 2008. In *Shadow of the Leopard*, she has been true to Henning Mankell's unblinking, sensitive approach to the realities of life in Mozambique. Anna lives in Scotland.

SECRETS
IN THE
FIRE

★ New York Public Library's Books for the Teen Age List
★ IRA Notable Books for Global Society Selection
★ SIG Notable Book
★ "The Year's Best" List, Resource Links

Based on the indomitable spirit of real-life landmine victim Sofia Alface.

"A hard-hitting, eye-opening novel that brings readers face-to-face with the horrors of war ... Mankell's language and style are spare, but elicit a deeply emotional response."
                    —*School Library Journal,* starred review

"One of the first books to dramatize the global landmine crisis for children, this docu-drama will grab readers with the truth of one child's terror and courage."
                    —*Booklist,* starred review